More Than a Voyeur

La Petite Mort Club Intimate Encounters, Volume 5

Ellis O. Day

Published by LSODea, 2024.

MORE THAN A VOYEUR

First edition. July 18, 2024.

Copyright © 2024 Ellis O. Day.

ISBN: 978-1960201188

Written by Ellis O. Day.

Also by Ellis O. Day

Six Nights Of Sin
Interviewing For Her Lover
Taking Control
School Fantasy
Master-Slave Fantasy
Punishment Fantasy
The Proposition

The Billionaire's Baby
The Baby Bargain
Making the Baby
The Baby Battle
Having The Baby

The Dom's Submission
His Sub
His Mission
His Submission

The Pleasure Associate
The New Hire
Becoming a Whore
Back to the Grinding

The Voyeur
The Voyeur
Watching the Voyeur

Touching the Voyeur
Loving the Voyeur

Standalone
The Dom's Birthday Weekend

Patrick and Annie's relationship is on the rocks.

He's happy with their sex life, but she's always been kinkier than him. He's sure she wants to add someone else to their bed.

He's had threesomes before. It's only fair that she gets to try one. It shouldn't be a big deal, but it is. He's not sure he can survive watching another man touch her, but he doesn't think their relationship will last if he doesn't allow her to experiment with more kink.

Annie's been in failed relationships before. She knows the signs and Patrick is sending them loud and clear, but she's not ready to let it end. She loves him too much.

When he suggests that they invite another person to their bed, will she agree? Does she want that?

If they go through with it, will it make their relationship better, or will it destroy it?

If you enjoy romantic comedies with explicit, kinky sex where two people work through their issues and end up a better couple, then you'll love More Than A Voyeur.

Join My Readers' Group and for a limited time get the entire Six Nights of Sin series for FREE.

Get your free book on my website.
www.EllisODay.com

1

CHAPTER 1: Patrick

Patrick turned off the car and stared at the wall of his garage. This was the first time since Annie had moved in with him that he'd dreaded going home. They'd had some rough patches before but nothing like this.

Things hadn't been great between them since the blowup with her brother Vic. His news tonight wasn't going to make it better, but sitting here wouldn't change anything. It'd only delay it. He got out of the car and walked into the house, smiling at Sophie's and Boomer's barks of joy as they raced to greet him. At least they were happy to see him.

"You may have to share the couch with me tonight." He bent, scratching Boomer behind his long, floppy hound dog ears while rubbing Sophie's belly as she dropped onto the floor and rolled over. She'd gotten so big. She'd been a sweet little puppy when Nick had brought her to La Petite Mort Club, but now she was a forty-pound gangly terror.

"Patrick, is that you?" Annie called out.

"Yeah." *Who the hell else would be coming in through the garage?* But he kept that question to himself. It'd only start another fight, and they were already in for a doozie once he told her what he'd done. "Dinner smells great."

He headed into the living room, the dogs trotting at his side. She was an excellent cook. His hand drifted over his stomach which wasn't as flat as it'd been before they'd met. Her food was the best he'd ever tasted. He used to work it off at the gym and in bed. Their sex life had been off the charts hot—at least to him—but not lately.

He started for the kitchen. She'd been working a lot, trying to get her catering business going, and when she was home, she was usually busy cooking something. He veered toward the small bar in the dining room next to the kitchen. Tonight, they were going to both need a drink. He'd make hers stronger than normal to help soften his news. He pulled his phone and keys from his pocket and put them in a bowl on the counter. "I'm going to make a drink. You want one?"

1

"Sure, but you'll have to help me drink it." Her voice came from behind him not from the kitchen.

He spun around and his knees shook as his gaze wandered over his wet dream come to life. She was stretched out on the couch, wearing nothing but a blindfold and handcuffs. His throat dried at the sight of her body—all that hot, warm skin, fragrant and waiting for him. Her nipples were already hard little buds and her small waist curved into large hips that a man could sink into. Her legs were slightly open, and he swore that was wetness glistening on the patch of hair between her thighs.

"I thought we could fuck before we eat." She smiled and her lips were so wide and lush.

"I think we'll both be eating something very soon." He kicked off his shoes as he walked to the couch. "Starting with me."

He grabbed her ankles, moving her legs before sitting sideways on the couch. He leaned in, kissing along the crease of her thighs. She moaned and wiggled as his lips moved toward her pussy. He paused, inhaling the musky scent of her arousal. Fuck. He'd missed this. They hadn't been completely celibate but lately sex had been infrequent and quick. His dick pressed at his zipper, but that was staying locked up for a bit. He licked upward, slipping his tongue between her folds, and teasing her clit.

She moaned, her mouth open and her chest heaving. "Please, Patrick. Fuck me."

"Later." He didn't want to hurry through this. After he told her his news, she might not let him touch her for a while, so he was going to get his fill.

CHAPTER 2: Annie

Annie moaned as her bound hands reached for Patrick.

"First, I'm going to bury my face in your pussy." He kissed her fingers before tossing her legs over his shoulders.

"Oh god, Patrick." The linen of his shirt felt rough on the sensitive skin of her thighs as his hot breath teased her swollen flesh.

"You're so beautiful." He spread her lower lips and licked up her slit, soft and teasing.

"More. Please." She squirmed, but his hands tightened on her legs, holding her in place as he continued to run his tongue along her pussy in soft strokes.

He traced the sides, dipping inside her for just a moment and then flicking her clit.

"Oh, God. Yes." Her body bucked, trying to get closer to the pleasure. "Again. Do it again. Please. I need you inside me when you do that. Please." She writhed under him. She needed him...his fingers...his cock...something inside her to ease the ache of emptiness.

He stilled, his hands squeezing her thighs almost to the point of pain before he let go and stood, walking away.

"Patrick?" She pushed the blindfold from her face and sat up. "What's the matter?" *What had she done now?*

Things had been off between them lately, and she wasn't sure why. She'd been working a lot, but they still had sex. Not as often as before but that was to be expected in a relationship, especially when they both worked long hours. It didn't bother her, but how he treated her after sex did. Instead of being close and feeling connected, he seemed distant. Her gut twisted. She'd been through this before. It was how it always started—the beginning of the end. She almost choked on a sob. She couldn't lose him. She loved him more than she'd ever thought she could love anyone, but she didn't know how to fix things because she had no idea what was wrong.

"I'm just doing what you asked." His tone was hard as he came out of their bedroom. "As always."

"What do you mean by that?" She instinctively braced herself. He'd never called her pushy or bossy, but he hadn't defended her when her brother had. Was he pulling away from her because she was too bossy?

"Put the blindfold back on and get on your knees." His green eyes were dark like the forest at night as they skimmed down her body.

Her gaze dropped to the bulge in his jeans. He wasn't distant or disinterested now, and the best way to show she wasn't always bossy was to obey. She licked her lips. She couldn't wait.

CHAPTER 3: Patrick

Patrick's cock almost burst through his pants as Annie climbed off the couch and got onto her knees before pulling down the blindfold. She was so amazing and always so fucking eager to play. He absolutely loved how adventurous she was, especially in the bedroom, but he hated that he wasn't sure he was enough for her anymore. She kept hinting at things. Even a contortionist couldn't eat her out and fuck her at the same time. Nope, that required two men or.... He placed the vibrator on the end table next to the couch. He hoped this would satisfy her, but he feared it wouldn't be enough for long. She wanted another man not a toy. He didn't think he could share her with anyone, but he couldn't lose her either.

"Patrick?" She tipped her head a little, causing her dark hair to fall around her shoulders and over her fabulous tits.

"Raise your hands." His voice was already rough with desire. She obeyed immediately which made his cock throb, but he had a cure for that. He grabbed her hands with one of his, holding them over her head as he stepped closer. He unzipped his pants and pulled out his dick, skimming it across her mouth and painting her lush red lips with his precum. Her tongue darted out, tasting him. He groaned. It felt so fucking good. "Want more?"

"Always." She smiled and opened her mouth wide, waiting for him.

"Fuck." His balls tightened as he slid the tip of his dick into her mouth. His eyes drifted partially shut with pleasure as she swirled her tongue around him, exploring his slit. It felt so fucking good. "Keep your arms up." He wrapped his other hand in her hair and thrust forward, sliding into her mouth.

She closed around him, sucking.

"Annie. Yes. Like that." He thrust gently as she sucked. He'd love to slide all the way down her tight throat and feel it closing around his cock, but he only did that when she controlled the pace. Right now, he needed to be in charge. He was losing her. She wanted more than him. She wanted to fuck other men. He couldn't let that happen. She was his. His! His thrusts became harder, and she gagged. "Sorry, babe." He pulled back, his hand stroking her hair.

She lifted off him, breathing heavily. "It's fine. Please." She opened her mouth, waiting for him.

He slid into her hot wetness again, just the tip, and she sucked like he was a fucking thick milkshake. His legs trembled as he grabbed her head, holding her in place. Her suction increased, making his balls tighten. It felt so damn good. "Annie." He panted. "I'm gonna come in your mouth."

She sucked harder, and he slipped over the edge, his eyes closing as his hips thrust, spilling his seed, and finding relief in the fact that right now, she was his and no one else's.

When he was done, he pulled out. He'd come hard, but it wouldn't be long before he'd be ready again, especially if he kept looking at her. She was a gorgeous hot mess—her hair tangled from his fingers, blindfolded, bound hands over her head, her chest heaving and his cum dribbling from her mouth. "Your turn."

CHAPTER 4: Annie

Annie squeaked when Patrick picked her up and dropped her onto the couch. He unhooked her handcuffs and then lifted her leg. She pushed up her blindfold and her body almost melted at the sight.

His face was tight with tension, and his green eyes were almost black from desire. Her gaze dropped to his pants. He'd zipped them up, and there was no longer a delicious bulge, but she knew him well enough to know that it'd be back soon. Nothing could keep him down. He clamped the cuff around her ankle.

"What are you doing?" Her arm and leg were now attached.

"That'll keep you open and my head safe." He glanced up at her, a spark of amusement in his eyes.

"I can't help it that I squeeze you. It's your fault. You're too damn good at this."

"And don't ever forget it." He swatted the side of her ass.

"Hey." The protest sounded as false as it was. She loved it when he got a little rough.

He leaned over her. "Hello, Annie. I forgot to say it when I came home."

"Hi." Her heart melted. She loved this man so much. She touched his face with her free hand. "I was waiting for you."

"I saw that." He smirked as his eyes drifted down her body, sending tingles everywhere they touched.

"Did you like my surprise?"

"Very much." He kissed her, his tongue exploring her mouth as his hands cupped her breasts.

She moaned as he kissed his way down her neck, touching that spot that seemed to be directly linked to her pussy. He lingered there, licking and sucking. She wiggled, needing more. "Please, Patrick." She was desperate for him.

He moved downward, pausing on her breasts. He pulled a nipple into his mouth.

"Oh...." she moaned as he sucked, the sensations making her body tighten and the juncture between her legs throb with need.

He bit her nipple, sending a spark of heat through her before soothing the sting with his tongue. She writhed as his hot mouth burned a path to her abdomen but then he stopped, staring at her pussy.

She reached for him, tangling her hand in his hair, and gently pushing him downward.

"Trying to give me a hint?" He looked up at her, grinning as his fingers skimmed up and down her inner thigh, getting closer and closer to where she ached for him.

"Yes, damn it. I need you to stop teasing me and get to it."

"Patience, love."

"You weren't saying that when I had your dick in my mouth."

"That was entirely different." He traced her pussy, but his touch was fleeting and way too light.

"How?" She shifted, trying to catch his finger, but he only grinned wider.

"It was me on the edge, not you." He chuckled.

"You're an ass."

"Yep"—he pushed the leg that wasn't bound to her hand farther from the other as he bent—"but you love that about me."

"That is not one of the qual...." Her words turned into a moan as his mouth lowered to her pussy, and he licked deep inside her. "Yesss. Oh, God. Yes." Her hand tangled in his hair, and her free leg dropped onto his shoulder, her foot trying to pull him closer. He was so good at this; she wanted to scream and weep.

A hum filled the room, and her body froze except for the pulse between her legs. That increased...A LOT. She knew that sound. "Patrick.... Oh, my...."

The vibration skimmed over her clit, and she almost shot off the couch.

"Hold still." His hot breath branded her skin as he rolled that toy over her pussy, teasing her swollen nub.

"Oh, oh...Patrick." She bucked, not sure if she was trying to get closer or away as pleasure danced with pain.

"Stop moving." He slapped her thigh as he yanked her leg off his shoulder. He bent it at the knee and tucked it against his chest before leaning forward and holding her down as he pushed the vibrator into her.

"Oh, oh." Slick from her juices it slid easily into her. He pulled out and then pushed it back inside, fucking her with the toy. She moaned, her body clamping on to it as the vibrations stroked her passion. It felt so good but not as good as him. He was bigger and hotter and better but then his mouth was on her clit. He sucked as he thrust the toy into her, in and out as his tongue teased her nub, flicking and then sucking.

It was too much. She bucked against his face. "Please." She panted. "I can't."

"You can and you will." He moved so fast she barely knew what'd happened. He dropped her leg as he unhooked her handcuffs. He used his body to keep her still as he lowered his mouth to her pussy again. He sucked her clit as he pressed a button, turning the vibrator up.

She screamed. Her body spasmed so hard it stilled and then shattered, her pelvis thrusting as her muscles squeezed that toy.

"Fuck that." He lifted off her, pulling the vibrator from her body and tossing it aside.

"No. Pat...rick." Her pussy clenched, but there was nothing there. She needed the toy...him...something inside her. She curled into a ball, almost weeping from the emptiness, but then he yanked her legs apart.

His dick, hot and hard, prodded at her opening. She gasped as he shoved inside, her body still tight from her orgasm.

"Open for me." His mouth came down on hers, his tongue invading.

She couldn't help but respond, her body softening for him. He pushed all the way into her. He was hot and thick, stretching her. "Oh fuck. You feel so good."

He grunted in her ear as he pumped into her. He was way past pretty words. This was what she loved best, him out of control because of her. She responded to his need, pulling him deeper with each thrust, her orgasm spiraling back to full swing.

She wrapped her arms around him. His shirt scratched her skin in a wonderful way as his hot breath came in desperate pants in her ear. His strong body rubbed along hers. He was everything and everywhere—above her, around her, inside her. He was hers. Her body tightened, clinging to him, and she gasped as she came, squeezing him and holding him tight.

He thrust into her over and over and then his body stiffened. He groaned as his hips slowed, emptying his desire inside of her.

CHAPTER 5: Annie

Annie's hand ran up and down Patrick's back, content to stay just like this, maybe forever. She kissed his ear. "I'll have to surprise you more often."

"Hmm." He grunted and then rolled off her.

That wasn't quite the reply she'd wanted, and her heart tore a little. He got up, pulling on his pants. This was how guys acted when they were done with a woman. Sure, they'd fuck her but after that they were distant. That little tear turned into a full fledge maiming. She stood.

"Where are you going?"

"To put on some clothes." It was bad enough he was acting like a dick. She didn't have to be naked while he did it.

"I'll get you that drink." He walked to the cabinet where they kept their liquor.

"Make it a double." She strode into their bedroom, trying to stay calm. Things hadn't been great lately, but maybe it wasn't over between them. No, forget that. If he kept acting like this, she'd end it. She didn't need to put up with him being an asshole. She grabbed a bra and put it on, but the snap wouldn't fasten. He'd broken it a few weeks ago when he'd been eager to fuck. "Damn him." She threw it across the room and dropped onto the bed, tears welling in her eyes. Who was she kidding? She wasn't going to end it. She still loved him. She'd truly thought that she'd finally found her happily ever after, but once again, she'd been wrong.

She stood and walked to the dresser, putting on a different bra and a clean pair of underwear. He could've had a bad day. *Weeks of bad days and he didn't talk to her about it? That wasn't good either.* She put on a T-shirt and a pair of shorts. What was wrong with her that made all the men in her life leave? She was a bit strong-willed and stubborn, but she was also loving and caring. She wiped the tears from her eyes. This was not her fault, and she was tired of playing these games with him. She needed an explanation for why he was acting like this, and she needed it now. She stormed into the living room.

"We need to talk." He sat on a chair across from the couch where they'd just made love.

Her heart froze. Those were the four worst words in the English language. She knew they'd been fighting a lot, but she hadn't thought it was over, not really. She'd suspected, but she hadn't truly believed it. She swallowed the knot of pain in her throat. She'd survive. She always did. "Where's my drink?" She was going to need it.

"There." He nodded to the end table by the couch, a distance from him that seemed like a mile. She sat and gulped down half of it.

"Shit." His eyes widened. "I hope the news isn't that bad."

"Just tell me. I'm in no mood to drag this out." She couldn't believe him. He was dumping her, and he *hoped* it wasn't that bad.

"What do you think I'm going to say?" He frowned.

"Nothing."

"It isn't nothing that makes you chug your drink." His eyes narrowed as he puzzled it out. He was a top-notch private investigator. He'd figure it out sooner rather than later.

"You said we needed to talk." She finished her drink and stood, walking across the room, and pouring another one. "It's no secret what those words mean in a relationship."

"You think I'm breaking up with you?"

She shrugged, but the surprise in his voice soothed her heart and her nerves.

"We just made love." He stared at her like he had no idea who she was.

She should keep her mouth shut and shrug, but she wasn't the kind of person to keep her thoughts to herself. "Yeah. That doesn't mean you weren't still going to end things."

"We're in a relationship. Hell, we're living together. And you think I'm the kind of guy who'd fuck you and dump you?"

"No." She didn't, not really but.... "I was naked, blindfolded, and handcuffed when you got home." She sent him a sheepish smile. "I guess I just thought you were a guy."

He grinned and her pussy clenched. She was such a slut with him. One glimpse of that sexy smile and his sparkling green eyes and she wanted to jump him.

"You do have a point."

"So, you would fuck me and dump me." She strolled over to him, enjoying how his eyes darkened with desire as he watched her hips sway.

"Maybe. If you were naked."

"Then you are that kind of guy." She stopped right in front of him.

His finger ran along the bottom of her shorts. "Like you said, I am a guy"—he leaned forward and kissed the path his finger took—"but I'm not *that* kind of guy. I'd wait until the next day to dump you."

"You are so gallant." She laughed.

"I try." He straightened, smirking at her.

She sat on his lap. "I'm glad we're not breaking up." *Really, really glad.*

"Me too." He kissed the side of her head, leaning back in the chair and holding her close.

This was the Patrick she knew. The man she loved. "Why were you upset earlier?"

"Hmm." He kissed her again and then he tensed. "I do have something I need to tell you."

"Okay." His tone made her nervous, but she could handle whatever it was as long as they were together. "You know you can tell me anything."

"I know, but you're not going to like it."

She touched his face—so dear, so loved—and kissed him softly. "Since you warmed me up with a fabulous orgasm. I'm sure it'll be fine."

He frowned. "I'm loaning your brother the money to buy Smitty's place. He's moving this week."

She jumped off his lap. She needed to be as far away from him as possible, or she'd kill him.

CHAPTER 6: Patrick

Patrick had seen people run from explosions and gunfire, but he'd never seen anyone move as fast as Annie. She'd practically leapt from his lap.

"You're doing what?" Her brown eyes flashed sparks of fury.

He wanted to cover his head and hide. He was a former Marine and this little woman scared the shit out of him. It wasn't her temper. Although sometimes, like right now, it did make him cringe. It was the thought that he might lose her that filled him with fear. Still, he couldn't back down on this. He owed it to Vic. "You heard me, Annie."

"No." She shook her head as if that would make him change his mind. "Call him and tell him that you came to your senses, and you're not giving him the money because that is bullshit crazy."

"I'm not doing that." He tossed back his drink. "Vic needs this."

"Vic needs to stay here."

"Annie, I know you love him, and you're worried about him but—"

"For good reason." She crossed her arms over her chest, and his mouth went dry.

He'd never tire of looking at her tits. Clothed or unclothed, they were fabulous.

She took a step closer, running her fingers over his chin and lifting his head. "My face is up here."

"Yeah, and it's lovely, but these are perfection." He grinned as he grabbed her breasts, hoping to charm her out of her snit.

"Now is not the time." She slapped his hands away.

"Shame." Apparently, she hadn't found that funny or flattering. He leaned back in his seat. It was going to be a long evening, but tonight would be even longer. He forced himself not to grin in anticipation. When Annie's passions flowed with anger or joy, she got horny. His dick began to rise at the thought of the sex they'd have later when they were both in bed. She'd want to be in charge, and that was more than fine with him.

"Please call him and tell him that you can't. That you won't." She went over to the bar and grabbed his phone from the bowl before walking back to the chair and holding it out for him. "You know as well as I do that he can't move away. It isn't safe for him."

"I don't know that, and neither do you." He took her hand, pulling her back to his lap.

"He's a recovering drug addict. You know how fast they can fall back into that habit." She lifted his hand and placed the phone in it. "Please, for me. Call him. Talk him out of this."

"I tried, but his mind is made up." He dropped the phone next to his glass on the table. "He said he explained to you why he wanted to move."

"He did." She wiggled off his lap. "And it's stupid."

"To you, maybe, but not to him." He loved her passion and her desire to take care of everyone, but sometimes she could be so obstinate about any idea that wasn't hers.

"I don't care. I just got him back. I can't lose him again." She wiped her eyes.

"Oh, Annie." He stood and pulled her into his arms. "You have to let him live his life."

"I...I can't." She sobbed against his chest. "I almost lost him."

"I know." He kissed the top of her head. "We'll go and visit him whenever you want."

"Not...good...enough." Her words hiccuped with her sobs. "He...can...pretend, and we won't know." She stared up at him. "Drug addicts know how to hide their addiction."

"I know, baby." He kissed her. "But we have to support him in this. He needs this."

"Why does he need to move across the country and live in a cabin in the woods? Explain that to me."

"It's not across the country. It's a few hours away."

"It may as well be. I won't see him enough to know if he's slipping and using drugs again."

"He needs space. To think. To heal." If Vic hadn't taken Patrick's place on that mission, it might be him fighting these demons. He owed Vic his life, and he'd do whatever he could to help.

"He has space. He has the entire house where we grew up."

"It's not enough. He needs to get away. To be on his own without someone watching over him all the time." His breath froze in his chest. He hadn't meant to repeat that.

She stiffened, stepping out of his arms. "So, he's doing this because he needs to get away from me."

He'd fucked up, but he wasn't going to lie to her. "Not just you." He winced at the look of shock and hurt on her face. "I'm sorry, but you're over there every day. He knows you search the house when he's not home."

"I do not."

He sighed. "He installed cameras."

"Why didn't you tell me he put cameras in the house?" Her face heated.

"I had no idea." At her raised brow and tapping foot, he amended. "Okay. He asked me what kind he should use, but I never knew—"

"How could you?" She stared at him like he'd picked his nose and ate the booger.

"How could I?" He was an easy-going guy but sometimes she pushed him too far. "How could you? Why didn't you tell me you were snooping through his stuff...every day. *Every day*, Annie. Do you have any idea how wrong that is? How insulting it is to him?"

"Not every day and I wasn't snooping." That damn foot of hers was tapping again. "I was making sure he wasn't doing drugs."

"By snooping through his things."

"How else was I supposed to know for sure? Ask him?"

"Well...yeah."

"Drug addicts lie." She poked him in the chest. "They lie to everyone."

"Not all of them. Not the ones who are recovering." He grabbed her finger. "And because you can't see that, can't trust him to do that, you pushed him too far."

"He can't move without the money." She glared up at him.

"I'm not changing my mind." He was not backing down on this.

"Why?"

"You know why. I owe him. Plus, if I didn't, he'd get it from Ethan."

"Ethan won't loan it to him."

"Yes, he will."

"No, he won't." Her arms crossed over her chest, but this time he barely even glanced.

"How do you know?" He wasn't sure he wanted to hear her answer.

"I asked him." She wouldn't meet his eyes. "Right after Smitty's funeral when Smitty's stupid son put that thought in Vic's head."

"You talked Ethan out of helping your brother." He loved that Annie cared so much that she was a bit of a busybody, but this was going too far.

"I didn't talk him out of it. I told him that Vic might be thinking about moving there and explained how stupid it'd be. He agreed with me."

"He did. Really? Did you tell him that you search your brother's things every day for drugs? That you call him every morning and evening to check up on him? That you stop by his house several times a week when he's home even if he says he's busy because you pretend that you need to pick up something you forgot over there?"

"No, because none of that has anything to do with this." Her chin jutted out stubbornly.

"Nothing to do with...." His mouth opened and shut. Sometimes she was unbelievable. "You're like his guard. Jesus, Annie, I don't blame him for wanting to move." As soon as he heard the words, he wanted to pull them back. The haunted look of hurt in her eyes tore him apart. "I didn't mean it like that."

"Then how did you mean it?" Her face was pale.

"I meant that your brother needs to be treated like an adult. Like a man."

"And a man needs his space." Her words were calm and thoughtful.

"Exactly." That had gone easier than he'd expected.

"That explains why you've been so distant lately."

"Me? Distant?" Damn, he should've known it was a trap. Arguments with Annie never dissipated so quickly.

"Yes." She poked his chest. "For weeks you've been pulling away from me."

"When?" He had so not been doing that.

"Today, for example."

"Today?" The issues they'd been having were her fault, not his. "We just fucked on the couch. How is that pulling away from you?"

"It's not the sex. It's what you do afterward."

"I made us each a drink." Now, he was confused.

"You jumped off me, got dressed, and raced to the bar to get away from me."

"I did not do that. I walked to the bar and made us a drink. That is not trying to get away from you."

"Stop denying it. I was there."

"So was I." He hated fighting with women. They were so illogical. Every little action was studied and analyzed, and they always, *always* came to the wrong conclusion.

"Stop denying what you did. As soon as you were done you got up and got dressed."

"Fine. I did do that, but it wasn't because I wanted to get away from you."

"Then why did you do it?"

"Because I knew we were going to fight over this Vic thing."

"You knew I'd be angry and upset, but you decided to loan him the money anyway without talking to me?" Her foot was going to tap a hole in the floor.

"Yes." He wasn't the bad guy in this situation.

"And you knew all this when you came home?"

"Yeah." He started to feel like he was walking into a trap.

"Is that why you were late?"

"No. Yeah." He frowned. "I hate fighting with you." He ran his hands up and down her arms.

"And you knew we'd fight and yet, that didn't stop you from fucking me and having me suck your dick."

"Ah...."

"Apparently, you are *that* kind of man." She stormed away.

"That's not fair. You were naked on the couch, wearing a blindfold and handcuffs. What man would turn that down?"

"One who wants to have sex sometime in the future." She shouted over her shoulder as she headed toward their bedroom.

"Oh great. Now, you're going to withhold sex." He followed her. "You said that was a stupid thing women did, and you'd never do it."

She pushed past him, his pillow, and a blanket in her hands. "That was before my boyfriend decided to pick my brother over me."

He took a deep breath. "Annie, he needs this." He knew that letting his temper take control never worked with her, but she was pushing him.

"And you're a man. So, you need your space too." She dropped the bedding on the couch. "Enjoy." She spun around and went into their bedroom, slamming the door behind her.

"Unfucking believable. You're being completely unreasonable."

"Unreasonable?" She flung open the door. "I'm not the one being unreasonable. You're being an ass." She grabbed her purse by the door.

"Where are you going?"

"Somewhere away from you." She slammed the door to the garage on the way out.

"Go." He yanked it open. "You're right. I do need my space because you're driving me fucking crazy."

CHAPTER 7: Patrick

"Shit-fuck!" Patrick slammed the door as Annie pulled her car out of the garage. Good. He was glad she'd left. He couldn't be around her right now. She drove him bat-shit crazy sometimes. He stormed over to the bar and poured a hefty shot of whiskey, taking a gulp before dropping his large frame onto the couch. He yanked his pillow out from under his ass. "Fuck that." He tossed it aside. "There's no way in hell I'm sleeping out here. If she doesn't want to sleep with me, she can take the couch."

Boomer crept from his bed in the corner, head down and tail between his legs.

"Shit. I'm sorry." He softened his tone. Sophie didn't care if he yelled, but Boomer was different. Patrick guessed that the dog hadn't had a good home before he'd ended up at the shelter. The hound was friendly and energetic, but he hated it when Patrick raised his voice. "Come here." He patted the couch.

Boomer's tail wagged between his legs.

"I swear. You're not in trouble." He patted the couch again, and Sophie hopped up beside him and licked his face. "You either, baby." He rubbed her ear.

Boomer hurried over, jumping up by Sophie, not wanting to miss out on the attention.

"That's a good boy. You don't need to be scared." He kissed the dog's head. "You didn't do anything wrong." He sneered as he took another sip of his drink. "I didn't do anything wrong either, and she sure got pissed at me, but I'm not like that. I don't get mad for no reason." He chose to ignore that it'd been him yelling at no one that'd scared the dog in the first place. That wasn't important.

Boomer flopped down on the couch, resting his large head on Patrick's lap. "That's right. Everything's okay." He hoped it was, but deep down he knew it wasn't. "We just get mad sometimes. You know how she can be."

Sophie whined, and both dogs stared at him. He was pretty sure there was a scolding in their soulful brown eyes.

"Don't look at me like that. She's the one at fault, not me. I had to loan her brother the money. He needs this." He dropped his head back on the couch. "I wish that were the only problem." He sat up, glancing at the dogs. "What am I going to do? I think she's getting bored with me."

Boomer groaned. It was probably because Patrick's finger hit that spot behind the dog's ear, but he was taking it as disbelief.

"I know, but you saw how she met me today. I mean, I love that she was so fucking hot for me, and it was a great surprise, but I think she wants more. She's so kinky and adventurous. I love that about her, but"—he lowered his voice—"I'm not that exciting. I don't want threesomes or orgies. I don't want to perform on stage. I just want to fuck her brains out. That was enough before, but now...I think she wants more."

The dog closed his eyes.

"What should I do?" He leaned forward, putting his head in his hands. He loved her, but if he didn't do something he was going to lose her. "I need to talk to someone about this." Someone who could give him advice.

Nick was away for the weekend with Sarah and her family. Ethan didn't like to hear anything about Annie and Patrick's sex life. Mattie was still at the age where he banged a different woman every night. Hunter and Mitch were on a case. He could talk to Adrian, but he wasn't in the mood for jokes. That left Terry. "I'd probably get better advice from you two." He patted the dogs. "Wait a minute. Terry and Maggie had been at the Club several months ago as Dom and sub. His friend wasn't into sharing his women, but he'd invited other men to watch because he thought it'd help Maggie. He might be the perfect guy to talk to about this. He grabbed his phone and texted Terry.

PATRICK: Hey, got a minute.

TERRY: What's up?

This was not a conversation to be had through texting.

PATRICK: Where are you?

TERRY: What are you, my mother?

Patrick's hand tightened around his phone. The guy could be such an ass.

PATRICK: I need to talk, and I'd rather it was in person.

TERRY: I was close. You may not be my mother, but you are a woman.

Unfucking believable. He started to type "go fuck yourself" when his phone beeped again.

TERRY: Everything okay?

"That's new," he mumbled to the dogs. "Terry never would've asked me that before he met Maggie." He stood. "The man just might be able to give me some decent advice."

PATRICK: Not really. Woman problems.

TERRY: I'm at the Club in the office with Ethan.

"Great. Just great." So much for talking to Terry, unless...

PATRICK: Can we meet somewhere else?

TERRY: Why?

PATRICK: Ethan doesn't like to hear anything about Annie and sex.

TERRY: Fuck him. Ethan can put on his big boy pants and deal with it. Come over. We can talk.

Terry was right. Annie was a grown woman not the little girl Ethan used to know. Patrick and Annie lived together. Hell, they hung out at the Club. It was no secret she was a voyeur, and they had kinky sex. Ethan would have to get over his brother-like issues about Annie and sex.

CHAPTER 8: Annie

Annie sat at Chelsea's house while her friend got ready to go out. "I haven't gone clubbing in forever."

"You're welcome to come with me." Chelsea pulled on a shiny little blue dress that highlighted her green eyes and red hair.

"Not exactly dressed for it." She'd been so mad she'd left in her old shorts and T-shirt. She hated fighting with Patrick, but she couldn't believe he'd done this to her and to Vic. "Plus, I'm not in the mood." She sipped her wine.

"Are you sure you don't want me to stay home?" Chelsea sat, putting on her jewelry—all costume, but pretty.

"No. I'll be fine."

"Of course, you will. You and Patrick are the best couple I know."

"We used to be, but I'm not so sure anymore." She sighed.

"Honey." Chelsea took her hand. "You need to give your brother some space. I can't believe you were spying on him." She laughed. "I bet he was furious when he saw those videos."

"Probably." She grinned. "But it serves him right. He scared me for so many years." She wiped tears from her eyes. "I'm so afraid that if he leaves, I'll lose him for good this time. He might start doing drugs again, and if I'm not around to catch it, he could die, or go back to the streets or—"

"Oh, Annie." Chelsea hugged her. "You need to let him move on from this."

"I know." She did, but it was so risky.

"Good. Then you and Patrick will make up soon." Chelsea stood and grabbed her shoes. "You may have to swallow your pride and apologize to him."

"I'm not doing that." Annie shook her head. "He should've spoken to me before agreeing to give Vic the money. We're a couple. That's what people in relationships do."

"Annie...." Chelsea frowned at her.

"Don't." She held up her hand. "I'm not apologizing, but...I might admit that he's right about Vic needing some space, and that maybe I overstepped when I snooped through his stuff."

"I'm sure Patrick will be thrilled to hear all that. The poor guy probably doesn't hear he's right very often."

"Am I really that bad?" She blinked back tears. "Oh God, I am. I'm overbearing and bossy, and that's why he doesn't love me anymore." She shuddered trying to hold back her sobs. "I don't blame him."

"What? No." Chelsea sat, wrapping her arms around Annie. "I was kidding. That's—"

Annie pulled from her grasp. "I'll mess up your dress."

"Don't be silly." Chelsea glanced at her shoulder where the blue of her dress was darker from Annie's tears. "I don't care about that."

"I do." Annie stood. "I should go. I don't want to ruin anyone else's life."

"Stop being so dramatic." Chelsea stood. "Stay right there." She hurried into the kitchen and came back with a dishtowel draped over her shoulder. "Now, come here." She opened her arms.

Annie couldn't help it; she fell into her friend's embrace. Chelsea had been the only one she'd been able to count on for years. Before she'd met Patrick she'd been so alone. Vic had been missing, her parents dead, and her other brothers lived so far away. "I...I'm a horrible person." She sobbed. She'd always been bossy. She'd had to be with five brothers.

"You are not." Chelsea stroked her hair. "You're the best person I know. You love everyone you meet. You're kind and fair." She kissed the side of Annie's head. "I love you like my sister."

"I...I love you too."

"You know I didn't mean anything bad about you, right?"

"Yeah, but it's true. I don't tell him he's right and—"

"It's probably because he isn't right, and you're not a liar."

Annie laughed, her sobs slowing. "No. I'm not."

"So." Chelsea stepped back, her hands still on Annie's shoulders. "Do you want to tell me what's really going on?"

"You...you need to go, don't you?" She wasn't sure she was ready to talk about this with her friend. Chelsea wouldn't let her give half an answer. When secrets were involved, the other woman was like a terrier after a rat.

"Nope." Chelsea grabbed her phone from the table.

"Don't cancel. I don't want to ruin your night."

"I'm not." Chelsea pressed some buttons. "I said I'd be a little late." She took Annie's hand and led her to the table. "Now, talk."

Annie sighed. "I don't know what's wrong, but he's acting differently than before."

"How?"

"It's hard to put into words."

"Are you sure you're not imagining it? I mean you two are living together now. Things aren't as easy as when you were just dating. He's busy. You've been super busy with starting your own business."

"I know, but it's not that. I grew up with five brothers. I know what it's like living with males. I don't expect the day-to-day part to be perfect."

"Then what is it?" asked Chelsea.

She really didn't want to admit this, but.... "The sex."

"Gone bad, huh?" Chelsea frowned, shaking her head. "It happens and it sucks. You have two choices. Fix it or dump him. Life's too short to live with mediocre sex."

"That's not what I meant." Annie smiled a little in memory of that last time. It'd been so hot she'd almost combusted. "The sex itself is still unbelievable, but after—"

"Please don't tell me you're crying because he doesn't want to cuddle?" Her friend gave her a disgusted look. "Men don't cuddle."

"Patrick did. He liked to hold me afterwards."

"He just said that." Chelsea snorted. "They'll say anything at first to make sure they get to have sex with you again."

"No, it's true. Even when I roll away, he follows me in his sleep. He always has to be touching me when we're in bed." She'd wake with his leg over hers or his hand on her breast. That was his favorite position, and he wasn't angling for sex because he was sound asleep. "I even tested him one night."

"You tested him?" Chelsea stared at her like she was crazy.

"Yeah, he was asleep, but he was holding me close. I carefully moved to my side of the bed. A few minutes later he rolled toward me, his hand searching the mattress until he found me."

"Aww. That's sweet."

"I know. I even went into the bathroom. At first his hand had searched the bed, but I waited until he finally moved back to his side."

"How very scientific of you to test various scenarios." Chelsea said it with a straight face, but her eyes sparkled with amusement.

"Shut up." She laughed. "Anyway, when I got back into bed within a few minutes he moved and put his hand on my boob." She tried to smile, but her lips quivered. "It's like I'm a magnet, and he's metal. I love being his magnet."

"Okay, so now he sleeps differently. You're making a big deal out of nothing."

"It's not that. When he's sleeping it's the same, but before he falls asleep, he's distant. The only time he holds me anymore is when he is sleeping."

"That's weird." Chelsea's lips pursed in thought.

"I know. It's like his subconscious still loves me, but his conscious doesn't."

"I'm sure that's not it." Chelsea grabbed Annie's glass, taking a sip. "Has he said anything?"

"No. He just seems different, especially after sex." She sighed. "I think...." She swallowed, trying to get past the lump of words she didn't want to say but had to. "I think he's tired of me. Of us." She blinked, but she couldn't stop the tears.

"No way." Chelsea frowned. "You two are perfect together."

"Not anymore."

"Hmm." Her friend had that look on her face that said she wanted to say something but wasn't sure she should.

"Just say it." She took her glass from her friend's hand and took a drink.

"Do you think he might want...more?"

"More what?"

"You know...in bed. Different things." Chelsea waved her hand.

"More kink?" Annie's mouth almost dropped open. They did *a lot* of things. "Like what?"

"I don't know. What don't you do that you think he might want to do?"

"I...I really have no idea. I'm willing to try anything he wants."

"Anything?" Chelsea's eyes widened.

"Yeah." Now she was nervous. So many people didn't understand kink.

"Like...what if he wanted you to do it with an animal or squish a gerbil or something?" Her friend's eyes were as wide as plates.

"He wouldn't want that." She finished the wine. "I wouldn't be with anyone who'd want something like that."

"Okay. Good."

"Stop looking at me like that. We don't do weird things." Not really. At least, it wasn't weird to them.

"Sure." Chelsea's tone dripped with sarcasm and humor. "That's what all the kinkies say."

"Kinkies?" She laughed. "Did you just make that up?"

"Yes, because I didn't want to call my best friend a freak."

"What we do doesn't hurt anyone, and you shouldn't knock it until you try it."

Chelsea leaned forward. "Get me into that Club, and I'm sure I'll change my mind." Her eyes grew dreamy. "All those hot, rich men. Yummy."

"You mean all those experienced men who only want one thing."

"So? If that's all I want, then we're good."

"I know you, honey." She took her friend's hand. "That's not all you want." Chelsea was a flirt, and that made people, especially men, think she'd be fine with casual sex, but her friend preferred relationships.

"How did this become about me?" Chelsea pulled her hand away. "We can worry about me when you take me to that Club."

"I tried getting you a guest pass, but Ethan isn't a fan of allowing non-members into the Club." At least not friends of hers.

"You'll wear him down eventually, and I'll get to see the Club." Chelsea grinned.

"I'll keep trying." She didn't think it'd work. Ethan had open nights, but the guests were supposed to be rich enough to afford a membership, and that wasn't Chelsea. Plus, she was pretty sure he'd denied her request because he was still miffed about her being at the Club. He still thought of her like his little sister at the age of ten.

"Great, but back to you." Chelsea walked to the refrigerator and grabbed the bottle of wine. "You said that you'll try whatever he wants." She rolled her eyes. "That means the important question is what would he be afraid to ask you to do?" She walked to the table and sat before refilling Annie's glass. "It must be something really weird. I mean, kinky."

"I don't think that's the issue. We've done"—she paused at the almost feral gleam of interest in her friend's eyes—"a lot of stuff. He shouldn't be afraid to ask me anything." Her body flushed at the thought of all the wonderful things he'd taught her.

"Like wh—" Chelsea's phone beeped. She looked at it, frowning.

"Everything okay?"

"Yeah. The club is packed. They're going somewhere else, but they haven't decided where."

"Go." Annie stood. "Have fun. I need to get home to the dogs anyway."

"Are you sure?" Chelsea hugged her. "I'll stay and hash this out with you."

"No. You gave me something to think about." She headed for the door.

"Call me tomorrow." Chelsea locked her apartment behind them. "And think about what you did right before he seemed upset or distant."

"I will." She didn't think that was it because she'd been naked on the couch, and she knew he'd enjoyed that.

CHAPTER 9: Annie

Annie pulled her car into the garage. It was empty. Patrick had left, but he didn't leave-leave, right? Her heart raced as she went into the house.

"Hey, babies." She patted the dogs who greeted her at the door with barks and wagging tails and then hurried toward their bedroom. She sighed, letting her world shift back into place when she saw that his things were still in the closet and on the dresser. He was coming back, unlike Vic who was running away from her.

Boomer nudged her hand.

"You need out?"

The dog put his wet nose in her palm, staring up at her with his soulful brown eyes. Unlike Sophie who was still such a puppy, Boomer was very sensitive to her feelings.

"Yeah. I'm upset, but it's not you. It's me." She laughed as she bent, rubbing his ears, and kissing his head. "Don't worry. I'm not breaking up with you." She wiped her eyes. "Hopefully, I'm not breaking up with anyone."

She changed into her pajamas and went into the living room. She poured a glass of wine and turned on some music, tossing Patrick's pillow and the blanket on the other end of the couch before sitting down. She checked her phone, but there wasn't a text or voicemail from Patrick. It was after eleven. She started to text him but stopped. She wasn't ready to see him right now anyway. She had to think. She took a sip of wine and rubbed Boomer's long, floppy ears as he jumped on the couch.

"What is wrong with him?" She glanced at the dog. "Does he confide in you?"

Sophie hopped up on her other side and rolled over, her pretty brown eyes staring up at Annie in adoration.

"Patrick used to look at me kind of like that, but now there are questions in his eyes." She rubbed Sophie's belly and dropped her head against the back of the couch. "I have no idea what he wants from me. I've tried everything he's ever asked me to do, and I've enjoyed it. All of it." She sat up, smiling as she sipped her wine. "I love doing things with him, but maybe I've been too easy. Guys get bored with easy women, right?"

Sophie wagged her tail, and Boomer nudged her arm, letting her know he wanted attention.

"Maybe he wants a challenge." She took another drink. "He didn't have to work too hard to get me today. Ha." Her laughter faded. "I just about jump that man every time I see him." She looked at the pup who now had her head on Annie's knee. "Don't look at me like that. It's not my fault. He's fricking gorgeous and so good at all those lovely, naughty things." A pulse beat between her legs just from thinking about him. She could crawl into their bed naked and wait. Even though they'd fought, he wouldn't stay on the couch. She smiled into her glass. "He couldn't reach my boobs from there so the poor man wouldn't be able to sleep."

Her phone beeped, and she grabbed it. She took a deep breath to hide her disappointment. "Hey, Chelsea."

"Hey. Are you doing okay?" Chelsea almost yelled to be heard over the loud music in the background.

"Yeah." She tried to sound happy but must've failed.

"You don't sound okay."

"I am. It's just…. He's not here."

"You did have a fight. You left. He left. Don't over think this."

"Yeah, but I went to see you. He probably went to the Club. That's full of gorgeous women who are there to have sex."

"But he went to see his friends." Chelsea moved a bit away from the pounding music. "Trust me. Patrick's not the cheating type."

"I guess." Her friend had the worst taste in men. All of Chelsea's boyfriends had cheated on her.

"Have you thought about what he might want to try with you?"

"I don't think that's it."

"Okay, Annie spill. I've known you too long. You think you know what the problem is, and I'm pretty sure you're wrong."

"Hey! Why would you say that? You haven't even heard it yet."

"Because you overthink everything when it comes to men and emotions. I keep telling you they aren't like us. They're simple beings." Chelsea laughed, saying something to someone. "Bobby agrees."

"Tell him I said hi." They'd all gone to culinary college together.

"Hi, Annie." Bobby was apparently now sharing Chelsea's phone.

"Hey." She smiled. "I miss you guys."

"You should come out with us sometime," he said.

"I should. I will." Just because she was in a relationship didn't mean she couldn't go out with her friends. Patrick had never said anything to suggest that he didn't want her to see them. She'd just started spending all her free time with him.

"So? What's your brilliant idea?" asked Chelsea.

"You're going to laugh." She really didn't want to tell them, but she would. Her friends looked at things differently than she did, and she needed to see this from all angles.

"Great. I need a good Annie-laugh," said Bobby.

"Very funny." They used to make fun of her stories when she'd been working as a maid at La Petite Mort Club.

"Go on," chided Chelsea.

"I think maybe I should make Patrick work for it a little more."

"It?" asked Bobby.

"You know, sex." She had no idea why she'd whispered the last word.

"Let me be clear." Bobby paused. He was so dramatic. "You're saying that you're putting out too easily and that he wants to have to earn it?" He could barely keep the laughter from his voice.

"It's not funny. I have been very...shall we say eager. Maybe even a little aggressive."

"Aggressive? Aggressive how?" asked Bobby. "I really, really need to know."

"It's none of your business." She was glad they were on the phone because her face had to be as red as a tomato.

"Come on," prodded Bobby. "You started this."

"Yeah, tell us. We need to know all the details." Chelsea laughed. "Okay, maybe not *all* the details, but we definitely have to know why you think you've been aggressive."

"Fine." She was pretty sure she was going to be sorry about telling them this. "When he came home today, I was waiting for him."

"So?" asked Bobby.

"How were you waiting?" Chelsea knew her so much better than Bobby.

"I was on the couch wearing nothing but a blindfold and handcuffs."

There was silence.

"I can't wait to tell Dave. He's going to be so upset that he didn't try harder to get you to go out with him," said Bobby.

"Dave and I are friends." Dave had flirted with her, but she'd never taken him seriously. "And he had a girlfriend."

"He would've dumped her earlier if he'd known how kinky you were. Hell, if I weren't gay, I'd be all over you." Bobby laughed.

"The point is that I think he's getting tired of me." Her heart spasmed like it was dying. Boomer nudged her, and she rubbed his ears. At least the dog still loved her.

"No. No way." Chelsea tried not to laugh. "No guy gets tired of a woman who greets him naked and handcuffed. Tell her, Bobby."

"You don't understand. He's had that kind of stuff for years at the Club, but...but with different women."

"She might have a point." said Bobby.

"What?" Chelsea almost shrieked.

"Some guys are assholes. Dave had a girlfriend who'd always been there for him, but he dumped her because he wanted more excitement. And Rick actually told me that he broke up with his girlfriend because he missed the chase."

"See. That's what I'm saying." She was happy Bobby was on her side, but she also hated it because that meant it was the end. She could make Patrick work for sex a bit more, but that'd never satisfy him long term.

"Dave and Rick are assholes," said Chelsea. "Patrick is not like that."

"He's not a jerk, but...." Damn, this hurt to say. "That doesn't mean he's not tired of me."

"If he is, leave his stupid ass," said Bobby. "He doesn't deserve you."

"He's right," said Chelsea. "Talk to him, and if that's his problem, pack your things and go."

"You're right." She blinked back tears as her heart shattered, but she'd been hurt before. This would not destroy her. "I'm not going to change. I'm not going to act like I don't like sex just because he wants some variety in his life. Asshole," she mumbled as she stood and walked over to the bar.

"Exactly," said Bobby.

"He can go back to paying for it." She filled her glass with more wine. "What a jerk."

"That's right," said Bobby. "Make the bastard pay you."

"I didn't mean me." She actually pulled her phone from her face and gave it a disgusted look.

"I'll never understand why women are so touchy about this shit," muttered Bobby.

"So, you'd let some guy pay you for sex?" Chelsea's voice was incredulous.

"Some guy like a forty-year-old pot-bellied non-bather? No, but some hot guy who I was attracted to...? Hell, yeah."

"You guys are the best." Annie laughed, feeling good for the first time in a long time.

"We love you, babe," said Bobby. "That's what friends are for."

"I feel a lot better now."

"Good. You should join us," said Chelsea.

"I should." She took a big gulp of her wine. "No. I am."

"Yay!" shouted Chelsea.

"Text me the name of the club. I'll be there in a few. I gotta shower quick and get dressed."

"And call an Uber," said Bobby.

"Exactly." She finished her drink. "See you soon." She hung up the phone. "Sophie, you're on his pillow."

The pup was lying on the couch with her butt right in the center of Patrick's pillow. Annie reached for it and then stopped. "You know what? Too bad. The jerk deserves some doggie butt juice on his handsome face." She turned and hurried into their room. She was going to go out, dance, laugh, and forget all about him, at least for a few hours.

CHAPTER 10: Patrick

Patrick tapped on Ethan's office door before walking inside. The outer office was empty, so he headed for the back room.

"About time." Terry threw his cards into the middle of the table.

"You can't just quit." Mattie glared at him.

"Sure, I can," said Terry. "Our friend is having some problems, and he needs our advice."

"But I would've won that round." Mattie looked to Ethan for the final say.

Nick's brother Mattie was in his late twenties, owned his own garage, and was the best mechanic around, but he was still so young at heart. The service had made Patrick grow up fast.

"He's allowed to quit," said Ethan.

"See." Terry grinned as he leaned in to collect his money.

"That ain't right, man." Mattie frowned, shaking his head.

"Sure, it is." Ethan stopped Terry's hand. "It's called folding."

"Shit." Terry leaned back. "Patrick, you just caused me to lose a thousand bucks. Pour me a drink."

"Excellent." Mattie looked at Ethan. "You're up."

"Fold." Ethan tossed his cards in the center of the table.

"Yesss." Mattie pulled in the pile of cash. He wasn't poor, but he didn't have the money to hang with Ethan and Terry like his brother Nick did.

Patrick wouldn't be surprised if Ethan had thrown in his hand to let Mattie win. He already gave him a discounted membership to the Club.

Patrick walked to the bar, poured himself a whiskey and soda, making it extra strong and then carried the scotch over and refilled Terry's drink. "Where's Maggie?"

"Home. Studying."

"And you left her to take care of the kids." He walked back to the bar.

"No." Terry gave him a disgusted look. "I'm not that much of an ass. They're with their father." His frown turned into a smirk. "And she said I was too much of a distraction, so she sent me out for a few hours." He took a sip of his scotch and sighed. "I have a fun night planned when I go home. She's going to get some more homework."

"And I'm sure you'll punish her for not doing it correctly." Ethan chuckled.

"Exactly. I'll watch over her shoulder the entire time she's doing it so I can catch every mistake."

"Anyone else want a refill?" He waited by the bar.

"Beer," said Mattie.

"Yeah." Ethan leaned back, tipping his chair. "So, what brings you here tonight?"

Patrick glanced at Terry who had a smirk like a cat who'd hacked up a hairball in a shoe. He filled Ethan's glass with brandy and handed Mattie a beer. "Terry didn't say anything to you?"

"He did." Ethan glanced across the table, wariness in his gaze. "He said that you were coming by, and you had a big announcement to make." He smiled. "The only big announcement I can think of is that you finally proposed and are going to stop raping Annie."

"Raping?" He sat on the couch. "I'm not raping her."

"That's the only excuse for what's happening because otherwise, I know she'd still be a virgin."

Mattie almost spit out his beer and Terry roared with laughter. Even Ethan couldn't quite keep his lips from twitching.

"The virgin voyeur. Sounds like a porn movie," said Terry.

"Do not mention her...hobbies." Ethan frowned.

"But they're so interesting." Terry grinned. "Usually, guys are the voyeurs, but little Annie"—he shook his head—"sure does like to watch." His eyes darted to Patrick. "And play as much as any of us."

"Shut the fuck up," said Ethan.

"Why? It's the truth." Terry's dark eyes gleamed with amusement. "You know I always speak the truth whether anyone likes it or not."

"I bet your daughter has some interesting secrets too. Maybe I should invite her to the Club. She's home from her European tour, right?" Ethan raised his brow at his friend.

"Not yet. She wanted to stay a little longer."

"I bet she did. All those foreign men with sexy accents." Ethan's blue eyes sparkled. "They're not nearly as hung up about sex as American men. Do you think she met a Dom or a new Daddy who loves teaching her not to be a bratty sub."

"My daughter isn't a brat." Terry was no longer amused.

"She is a bit spoiled." Patrick enjoyed messing with Terry as much as Ethan did.

"She is not spoiled. She's an intelligent woman who knows what she wants and doesn't settle for anything else."

"And it seems"—Ethan shot Patrick an amused glance—"she wants a big European cock."

Terry shrugged. "She's in her twenties. I'm under no illusions that she's a virgin."

"I can't believe that doesn't bother you," said Ethan.

"She's an adult. As long as she's careful she can do what she wants." Terry sipped his drink.

"Hmm. That's very mature of you," said Ethan.

Terry nodded like a fucking king.

"Just one question." Ethan leaned forward. "Why are you clutching your glass so tight that your knuckles are turning white?"

Terry's eyes locked with Ethan's. "Because I'm imagining it's your fucking neck."

"I knew it." Ethan roared with laughter.

"Yes, it bothers me to even think about what those fucking assholes are doing to her."

"Or to her asshole," muttered Mattie.

The room fell silent as the three looked at him.

"What?" Terry's dark eyes were deadly.

"That's his daughter." Ethan punched Mattie's shoulder. "Have some class." He sent Patrick an amused glance. Fucking with Mattie was their new favorite game.

"Sorry," Mattie mumbled and took a long gulp of his beer.

"So...." Terry turned to him. "All joking aside, what's going on with you and Annie."

Patrick looked at Ethan. "You may want to go into the business part of the Club."

"And leave you here to get advice from Terry and Mattie? Annie is closer to me than my own sisters. I wouldn't do that to her."

Patrick was a bit relieved. Terry was super controlling, and Patrick didn't roll that way, and Mattie changed women more often than his shop changed oil.

"Hey. My relationship is going great. Better than great." Terry stared at his drink, a soft smile on his lips.

"And you're welcome for that." Ethan sat a little straighter.

"For what?" Terry gave his friend a disgusted look.

"For this." Ethan threw his arms out. "The Club."

"Fine. Thank you for the Club. Without it I wouldn't have met Maggie." Terry looked at Patrick and rolled his eyes.

"You're welcome for that too."

"Too?"

"Yeah. I meant for the weekend the two of you spent here."

"We were happy before we did that."

"But not as happy as afterward." Ethan smirked. "I swear after that weekend you two looked like teenagers with their first crush."

"It was a good weekend." Terry's smile deepened a bit.

"You're actually blushing." Mattie leaned forward.

"Stop looking at me like that." Terry frowned at him.

"Can't. I never thought I'd see the day Terry the Dom was tamed. It's magical. Like looking at a unicorn." Mattie stared at Terry with fake awe.

"A unicorn who's thankful his horn is stiff once again," muttered Ethan.

"One time." Terry almost growled. "You jackasses shouldn't have been watching."

"We were trying to keep you from making a big mistake," said Patrick.

"But your dick did that for us," laughed Ethan.

"Enough." Terry held up his hand. "Our friend is having woman troubles, and you guys are joking. Shame on you."

"Fuck off." Ethan snorted. "You're pissed because we're laughing at you."

"No. I'm a better friend than you are." Terry sat up straighter, a smug expression on his face.

"Actually," Patrick leaned forward. "I'd like to talk to you about that weekend you spent here with Maggie."

"What about it?" Terry's face was guarded as he leaned back in his chair.

"I was wondering...I mean I heard...." How did he ask Terry about this? They joked, but they never really talked about their relationships and feelings. They were men, not women.

"Spit it out," said Terry.

"I think Annie wants to see...." He hesitated. That wasn't quite right. She wanted to fuck someone else not see them, but he just couldn't say that out loud. "Other men."

"Ah, shit. Man, I'm sorry." Ethan walked to the bar and brought over the bottle of whiskey, filling Patrick's glass.

"Did she say that?" asked Terry.

"Not in so many words." He chugged some of his drink. "But she may as well have."

"What words did she use?" Terry's dark eyes studied him.

"Just because you're a lawyer and you need the words spoken out loud doesn't mean that it's the only way people say things." He'd been dumped before; he knew the signs.

"I believe it's actually the definition of the word say."

"Stop being an ass. She's let me know in other ways."

"How?" Terry took a sip of his drink. "I'm not trying to be an ass, but actions can be misinterpreted."

"I'm not misinterpreting." He took another gulp of his drink.

"Explain," said Terry.

"Shit. By the look on Patrick's face, I don't think I want to hear this," mumbled Ethan.

"Go on," prodded Terry. "Ethan is a big boy. He can handle it or leave."

"It's my fucking office." Ethan took a gulp of his drink as he waved his hand for Patrick to speak.

"Well, you know she likes to watch and"—he glanced at Ethan—"I go with her, and we...do...things."

Ethan's eyes hardened, but he nodded at Patrick's vagueness.

"You knew she was a voyeur when you started dating her," said Terry. "It's not fair to her if that's suddenly a problem."

"It's not. Trust me. That is not our problem." Fuck. The last time they'd come to the Club it'd been so hot. They'd watched Cindy again with her multiple lovers, and Annie had been raring to go. They'd both come and then they'd sit there, watching and relaxing while Cindy would go at it again. It'd made them both so horny, that they'd fucked again and again.

"Wipe that look off your face, or I'll do it for you," Ethan glared at him.

"I didn't say anything." He tried to look innocent, but he was pretty sure he had failed.

"But you were thinking about it."

"I was remembering a...pleasant time Annie and I had here."

"Don't. Don't say another fucking word," growled Ethan. "She's like my sister."

"But she's not," said Terry.

"So," said Mattie. "I'm siding with Ethan here."

"Surprise, surprise," mumbled Terry.

Mattie had become Ethan's new sidekick.

"Nick is much more mature about his sisters than you are," said Terry. "He understands that they're grown women with needs."

"Shut up. Nick is wrong. Our sisters do not have needs." Mattie frowned at his beer.

"Right." Terry laughed. "And their husbands stay with them why?"

"I'm not here to talk about my sisters." Mattie stood. "I'm going into the Club."

"I'll join you." Ethan slapped Patrick on the back. "Give Annie my apologies for all the shit advice he"—he looked at Terry—"is going to give you, but I can't sit here and listen to you talk about her and sex. I just can't." He and Mattie headed for the door.

"Sure." He was a little disappointed, but ever since that thing with Liv had ended, his friend had been different. He was actually glad to see Ethan going back into the Club and socializing.

"Now that the big baby is gone, if you don't mind Annie's desire to watch, what exactly is the problem?" asked Terry.

"I don't care that she's a voyeur, but...it's what she wants to watch."

"What does that mean?"

"She...." God, this hurt to say out loud. "She always picks scenes with more than one guy."

"Hmm." Terry's face scrunched in thought. "She never picks anything else?"

"Sometimes, but not usually."

"A lot of scenes here are like that."

"There are plenty with one guy and more than one female or with just a couple."

"Yeah, but I'm guessing straight women would rather watch more guys than more women." Terry took a sip of his drink. "Have you talked to her about it?"

"Not yet." He finished his drink. "You know me. I don't like threesomes. Never have."

"Me either."

"How did you handle those other guys and Maggie."

"I didn't let them touch her, that's how." Terry's voice was gruff with annoyance.

"What if she had wanted them to?"

"She didn't." Now his tone was pure Dom—arrogant know-it-all.

"How do you know for sure?"

Terry was silent for a long minute. "I asked her."

"Wow." Patrick leaned back in his seat. He'd kind of figured that Terry would've just told her. "What would you have done if she'd said she'd wanted them to touch her? To fuck her."

Terry tossed back his drink before walking to the bar and refilling it. He sat back down, his face tight with determination. "I would've let them."

"Really? You? You never share."

He studied Patrick for a long moment. "I love her. I'd do whatever I have to do to make her happy."

"Even share her?"

"On occasion, if that was what she wanted." He took a large gulp of his drink.

"You were lucky that she didn't. I just...I just don't know if I can."

"Stop. Enough." Ethan walked back into the office.

"We'll stop talking until you leave." Patrick needed to gather his thoughts anyway.

"No. Moron. I heard everything. I was standing in the outer office."

"I thought you left." Patrick glanced at Terry who seemed as confused as he was.

"I couldn't. I love her like a sister and"—Ethan looked away, his face pinched like he'd eaten something sour—"as much as I'm pissed that you fucked her when I told you to keep her out of trouble, you're good for her, and she's good for you."

"Thank you." He was touched. His friend hadn't been happy about them getting together.

"Just shut up and listen." Ethan poured himself a brandy and tossed it back. "I can't believe I'm going to do this." He refilled his glass and then sat, taking another long drink. "It doesn't matter if she wants another guy as long as she wants him with you." His eyes bore into Patrick's. "She does want you there too, right?"

"Yeah...I think so." He dropped his head on the table. "Fuck, Ethan. Now, I have another thing to worry about." What if she didn't want him at all? She still desired him, but maybe she wanted an open relationship. He didn't think he could do that.

"Don't worry about it. Ask her," said Ethan.

"I can't. Not until I know what I'll do if she says she wants other men to fuck her, with or without me." He lifted his head. "I have to be prepared." They'd both been in the service. Ethan would understand that.

"Okay, let's tackle the first scenario." Ethan shoved his shoulder. "And stop looking like your dog died. You're a fucking Marine for Christ's sake."

"You're right. I can handle whatever it is." He wasn't sure about this though. His body and mind could handle anything, but his heart had always been his weakness.

"So, Annie wants a threesome," said Ethan. "Who cares? You've had threesomes before. Let her try one."

"Don't give me that shit." A few months ago, he would've believed Ethan meant this, but not now. "You were furious when Liv—"

"Do not go there." Ethan's eyes narrowed. "If you do, this conversation is done."

"Fine." He knew that look in his friend's eyes. Once Ethan drew a line, he'd die on it. "But stop pretending that it doesn't matter who a woman fucks. It may not if you're just sleeping with her, but it makes a huge difference if you love her." He was pretty sure his friend understood that too well. Ethan hadn't been the same since Liv moved out of his place.

"Get over it. Who are you to tell her"—a muscle in Ethan's cheek spasmed—"what she wants sexually?"

"But the thought of another guy touching her makes me want to kill someone."

"But she loves *you*," said Ethan.

"Then why does she want some other guy's dick in her." God, he wanted to yank out his hair or tie Annie up and never let her leave him.

"Listen to me. She's younger than you. She's less experienced. She may want to try things that you've already done. There is nothing wrong with that."

"I don't want to lose her, but I don't think I can share her." His shoulders slumped.

"Fine." Ethan looked to the heavens for guidance. "I'm going to bring up some things that I really don't want to talk about."

"Okay." Now he was nervous. They talked about pretty much everything.

"I'm sure you and Annie do some...interesting things at the Club." Ethan picked up his glass. "You're both here often enough."

"Yeah, we are." Patrick smiled. He loved that Annie was so open and kinky. He just wished she didn't want to be open and kinky with another man.

"What if you invite a woman to the bed instead of a man," interrupted Terry. "It's still a threesome, but you aren't quite so redundant."

"He has a point, but that also has its risks," said Ethan. "The concept is much more appealing, unless you discover that she prefers the woman over you."

"Good point." Terry frowned and took a sip of his drink. "Then you're worse than redundant; you're obsolete."

"I don't think that'd work. Annie never wants to watch two women and very seldom two women and one guy." He refilled his glass. "Nope. It's another man she wants."

"Let's say you're right and that Annie does want to invite another man to your bed," said Ethan.

He hated even thinking about it, but he would.

"Do you think she has anyone in mind?" asked Terry.

Patrick frowned. The scenes they'd watched never starred the same people too often, and he hadn't seen her talking to any particular guy. "I don't think so."

"Good, then she probably just wants to experiment, not replace you," said Ethan.

"You think?" Maybe it was the alcohol, but that did kind of make sense.

"I disagree," said Terry. "If a woman is interested in another man or a woman, you'll be the last to know."

"Not every woman cheats like your ex," said Ethan.

"Maggie's ex cheated too," said Terry.

"Maggie's ex was a guy." Ethan tipped his glass like he'd scored a verbal point.

"He still cheated. Stupid bastard." Terry hesitated. "But I'm glad he's a stupid bastard."

"All of this wanting a threesome is your fault, Patrick." Ethan shook his head.

"How do you figure that?"

"You showed Annie that it was okay to watch and to try new things sexually." Ethan shivered. "You should've waited to touch her until after you got married and even then, just to procreate." He smirked. "Or better yet, you should've never touched her and just adopted babies."

"What?" Patrick's mouth literally dropped open.

"Good lord, Ethan. You are one messed up fucker." Terry laughed. "On one hand you think that everyone should fuck anyone they want—"

"As long as it's consensual," interrupted Ethan.

"Whatever." Terry continued, "It's all an excellent fuck-fest, but on the other hand if a woman is like your sister—not even your actual sister—she should be a virgin and stay a virgin even after she marries."

"And why is that a problem?" Ethan leaned back in his chair, smiling. "You forget. I know what fuckers like us do with women." He shook his head. "I can't believe you're okay with your daughter doing things like this."

"I'm not, but I'm a realist. She's not going to stay a virgin."

"Stay? She's running around Europe with friends. That horse has left the barn." Ethan snorted.

Terry's jaw clenched. "Yes, I'm aware of that, but as I was saying. Whatever she does, I don't have to know or think about it, unless you bring it up." He glared at Ethan. "So, stop."

"Fine." Ethan laughed. "Let's get back to Patrick's problem."

"Yes, and you're not helping him." Terry crossed his arms over his chest. "I'm changing my advice. Don't ask Annie anything. Take a vibrator or dildo to bed with you and fuck her until she can't walk straight."

"I'm not hearing this." Ethan put his fingers in his ears.

"I did but...I just can't stop thinking about it. I love her. I want her to be happy."

"And you're sure you can't do that for her?" asked Terry.

"Not in this case."

"Like I said, his fault." Ethan dropped his hands from his head. "He showed her what kink was. All sorts of it and now she wants to experiment." He took a sip of his drink. "I say, let her. Be there with her and help her enjoy it." He grinned. "But not too much unless you want a permanent threesome."

"I don't want one at all."

"Then wait it out and eventually you can break up." Ethan looked a little too happy about that.

"I don't want that either."

"I know." The laughter left Ethan's eyes. "And enough of this bullshit. I'm sure you like some things that Annie's not thrilled about doing but she does them because she loves you, and you like them."

"No." He shook his head. "She likes everything we do."

"Really? Nothing? There's not one thing you like more than her?" Ethan had a disgusted look on his face that any other time would've made Patrick laugh.

"No." He frowned. "I wouldn't ask her to do anything that she didn't enjoy."

"I didn't say she didn't like it at all. I said she didn't care for it as much as you do. I know you're not an ass. Everything is consensual, but we've all been with women who didn't really enjoy giving head but—"

"Annie likes doing that." He couldn't stop the slight smile. "A lot."

"I don't need you to answer out loud." Ethan's face darkened.

"Actually, there is one thing."

"Keep it to yourself," said Ethan.

"She's okay with—"

Ethan leaned across the table, slapping his hand over Patrick's mouth. "I said not to say the shit out loud."

He shoved Ethan's hand aside. "Sorry."

"It's your own fault." Terry laughed.

Ethan glared at Terry.

"He's drunk." Terry nodded at Patrick. "Any thought that drops into his head is coming out of his mouth."

"I don't care." Ethan turned back toward Patrick. "Whatever it is, she does it because you like it. You're surely a big enough man to return the favor with a threesome once in a while."

Ethan had a point. Annie really didn't care to play the submissive, but she did it for him. Still, he wasn't sure he could handle another man touching her, even occasionally.

"It's either that or eventually lose her," prodded Ethan. "Your choice."

He could do it. It'd kill him, but for her he'd bring another man to their bed. "Okay. I'll give it a try." He tossed back his drink. "Thanks."

"Wait a minute," said Terry.

"What?" He was pretty sure he couldn't take much more.

"You need to control this. You said you don't think she has her eye on anyone in particular so you should suggest someone."

"Me?" He pointed at his chest. He didn't want to pick the guy who'd fuck the woman he loved.

"That's good advice," said Ethan. "You don't want a guy who's better in bed than you."

"Or one with a bigger dick than yours," said Terry.

Ethan stiffened a little before adding, "Right. You don't want to pick your replacement."

"And"—Terry stood and began to pace—"you don't want someone that she or you will see all the time."

"I definitely don't want that." He might kill the guy.

"But you don't want some newbie off the street either," said Ethan.

"Why not?" A stranger off the street sounded fine to him.

"That could be dangerous," said Terry.

"He has to know the rules," said Ethan. "He needs to understand that you're in charge of the scene. She belongs to you."

"She doesn't belong to me."

"She does in that bedroom," said Ethan. "She's yours to protect, and you don't want some guy who's never done a Devil's Threesome."

"Right," said Terry "You want to make it good for her but not too good."

"That seems a little dishonest." He didn't want to do this at all, but he couldn't deceive her.

"Do you want a threesome all the time?" asked Terry.

"No." He couldn't do that. It'd kill their relationship.

"Then you don't want it to be too good," said Terry.

"Basically, you want it to bring you two closer." Ethan's eyes lit up. "And I know who'd be perfect for this."

"You already have someone picked out?" This was moving faster than he'd expected or wanted.

"Who?" asked Terry.

"Lee," said Ethan. "I think he'd be perfect."

"Lee?" Patrick was a little appalled. He didn't want Annie leaving him for this other guy but.... "The short, fat banker who comes almost before he gets it out of his pants?"

"No." Ethan gave him a disgusted look. "Lee from Texas."

"Oh, that Lee." Terry leaned forward. "Yeah. He'd be perfect."

"Lee? From Texas? No." He shook his head. Women loved Lee. He was rich, attractive, and that drawl of his with the cowboy swagger was an aphrodisiac. Annie would be sighing about the man forever. "That won't work."

"Why?" asked Ethan. "He's attractive, familiar with the scene, and not looking for a permanent threesome."

"And best of all," added Terry. "The guy is only in town a couple of times a year which means if she enjoys it, you'd only have to do a threesome twice a year."

"That's a good point." He leaned back on the couch. "A very good point." He could deal with a threesome for her once or twice a year or at least he hoped he could.

"Then it's settled." Terry tipped his glass. "You can talk to Lee the next time he's in town."

"Yeah. I can." He'd heard Lee had been in town a few months ago, so he had some time to prepare for this.

"Great. He'll be here tomorrow," said Ethan. "You want me to give him your number when I see him?"

"Tomorrow?" Fuck. He was not ready for this.

"You're a mean motherfucker, Ethan." Terry laughed. "Remind me never to date anyone you care about."

"What?" Ethan looked offended. "He needed some advice. I gave it to him and helped him pick the perfect guy."

"Yeah, and you gave him no time to prepare. We all know Lee's only around for a week or two. Not exactly a long time for Patrick to get used to the idea."

"Not my problem." Ethan's eyes sparkled with amusement.

"Wasn't Lee just in town?" Patrick scrambled for any reason not to go through with this.

"Yeah," said Ethan. "He's actually been coming here a little more often lately."

"Then he's not the perfect guy for this." Patrick was relieved.

"Yes, he is," argued Ethan. "He's still only here every couple of months which is better than most of the members."

"True," said Terry. "But not ideal. Why is he suddenly coming into town more often? Is he opening another branch of his business here?"

"He's not here for business." Ethan sipped his drink.

"Then why is he coming into town?" Patrick needed a good reason to look for someone else because Ethan was right; Lee would be perfect.

"He's infatuated with Desiree. The guy's got it bad. He's making a fool of himself because she made it very clear that she's not interested in becoming his lover outside of the Club."

"She's a smart, beautiful woman. If he's that hot for her, why isn't she angling for a more permanent position?" asked Terry.

"Like his wife?" Ethan sounded shocked.

"Other Pleasure Associates have captured that ring, and they were far less ambitious and gorgeous than Desiree," said Terry.

"First, Desiree isn't at all interested in marriage and second, Lee's momma would never let that happen." Ethan chuckled.

"He's a grown man," said Terry.

"Yes, but his mother is...." Ethan shook his head. "I don't know quite how to explain her. I've met many, many powerful people because of this place. I've had to convince a lot of them that this was a good thing for the area. It always took some concessions on my part, but when Mrs. Manning came to talk to me, I knew I'd met my match. She was sweet as sugar, but there was steel in her bones. Luckily for me, she was more than happy to let her boy keep his membership since I'm so careful about birth control and STDs." He laughed. "Her generation is fine with boys being boys as long as they do their duty for their family."

"Lee brought his mother to the Club to approve?" Terry's face scrunched up with disgust.

"No." Ethan grinned. "Lee doesn't know that she came to see me. Apparently, she has friends in the area who tattled on him. She tried to force me to cancel his membership. I talked her into meeting."

"If he really wants Desiree, he won't let anything stop him, especially not his mother." Terry snorted. "He's a man for fuck's sake, not a boy."

"True, but you never met his mother. You'd like her." Ethan smirked. "She's about as blunt as you, except she makes it sound so sweet."

"That's definitely not Terry." Patrick laughed.

"I should call her and see if she'll give you some lessons," teased Ethan.

"I don't need lessons. I'm fine how I am." Terry's eyes gleamed as he looked at Patrick. "You should rent a room at the Club. You don't want to bring a guy to your bed."

"Wait a minute." Ethan held up his hand. "This is not happening here. I don't want to know anything about it."

"He can't do this at his place," argued Terry. "He'd never get that image out of his head."

"I don't give a fuck. Go to a hotel."

"The Club is safer." Terry smirked. "And Ethan can sit here and watch Annie, his little sister, taking it from two guys and loving every fucking minute."

"Do you want to punch him first, or can I?" Ethan looked at Patrick.

"Me." This was the first time he and Ethan had been on the same page about Annie since Patrick had met her.

Terry laughed. "So glad you came to me for advice. This was fun."

Patrick now understood why Nick always said he needed new friends.

CHAPTER 11: Patrick

No matter how hard Patrick tried, he couldn't fall asleep. It was almost three A.M. Where the fuck was Annie? He grabbed his phone from the nightstand and texted her.

PATRICK: Where are you?

He stared at the phone, willing a message to appear but nothing did. What if something had happened to her? Car accident. Kidnapped. He sat up, turned on the lamp on the nightstand and scrolled through his texts. She didn't go see Sarah because she and Nick were out of town. Maggie had class tonight. Chelsea? Fuck, he hoped not. He liked Chelsea, but the woman was a flirt and single. Still, she was a good friend of Annie's, and they worked together. He started to text her when the dogs ran out of the bedroom, barking. Their tone was both happy and excited. He got out of bed and followed them. He glanced out the window. There was a strange car in their driveway.

"Shhh," whispered Annie to the dogs as she stumbled into the house. "I don't want to wake him."

It was the loudest whisper he'd ever heard, which meant she was drunk.

"Why?" asked a guy. "It'd serve him right to get woken up."

Patrick's fists clenched at the sound of the man's voice.

"Stop it, Dave." Annie laughed, wobbling a bit as the dogs jockeyed for the best position to get petted.

Dave. It figured. That guy had liked her for years, but he was no threat...unless she wanted someone a little closer to her age.

"Boomer, be careful." She staggered as the large mutt rammed into her legs. "Sophie, stop." She dropped her keys as the other dog jumped on her, almost knocking her down.

"Whoa." Dave's arms wrapped around Annie, catching her before she fell.

"Get your hands off her." He hadn't meant to say anything. He knew the kid was just trying to keep her from falling, but as usual, jealousy had annihilated logic.

"Oh," she squeaked as she jumped, throwing Dave off balance because the guy was just as drunk as she was.

"Shit," Dave yelled as they both tumbled to the floor.

Annie's burst of giggles filled the room as the dogs circled the two of them, licking them both. He hadn't heard her laugh like this in months, and it irritated him that another man was the reason she was having so much fun.

"Eww. Dog breath." Dave laughed, petting Sophie.

"Get up." He walked over to them.

"Patrick? You're home." She grinned at him from the floor.

"Time for me to leave." Dave scrambled to his feet.

Patrick wanted to punch the kid but instead said, "You didn't drive, did you?" He didn't like the guy, but he couldn't let him drive in this condition. He took Annie's hand and pulled her to her feet.

"Me?" Dave pointed at his chest. "No. No way." He laughed. "I'm wasted." He tipped his head toward the door. "Uber. They're great."

"Good." Now he went back to wanting to punch the kid.

"I love Ubers," said Dave. "The drivers are friendly, and you can drink as much—"

"Why are you still here?" He walked toward the kid, glaring at him.

"Patrick." Annie slapped his arm. "That's rude."

He shrugged. "So is staying out all night and not letting me know where you were."

"That's my cue." Dave slipped out the door.

"*Me*? You're mad at *me* for not telling you where *I* was?"

"Yep." He strode toward her. She could stress all the words she wanted. He didn't care. She was the one who'd been wrong, not him.

"Bullshit. This is your fault." She staggered to their bedroom.

"How is *you* going out and getting drunk my fault?" He followed her.

"You...you...." She almost fell trying to take off her shoes. Instead, she dropped on the bed, swinging her leg until the heels flew from her feet. "Because you left."

"You left first."

"You were...are a jerk." She reached behind her back, trying to unzip her dress, but she couldn't get hold of the zipper.

He should let her struggle, but he couldn't. He'd do anything for her. Anything. He sighed. He sat on the bed next to her. "Here. Let me help."

She dropped her hand to her side.

He slowly unzipped her dress, taking in all that lovely, smooth skin. His mouth watered, begging him to taste her. He leaned a little closer, letting his breath tickle across her back. She shivered but didn't move away. They were fighting. She was still mad at him, but worse than that, she was drunk. He should wait until she was sober, until he knew she wanted this, but his finger trailed down the exposed skin. She leaned back just a little, pressing into his touch.

"Move your hair." His voice was thick with desire and his dick already tented his sweatpants.

She lifted her arms, holding up her hair. It was thick and black like a night with no stars. It felt like silk sliding across his naked flesh. His lips found her neck, and she dropped her hair, grabbing his head and holding him close.

He needed to be inside her now. His hand trailed up her thighs, pushing the short dress out of his way. She opened her legs, giving him more access.

He slid his hand between her thighs, his fingers stroking across her underwear. "You're so wet."

"Patrick." She leaned back, kissing the side of his face.

"Were you dancing with Dave?" Was that why she was wet and needy? Had she been rubbing on that guy for hours?

"Yes." She tried to turn in his arms, but he grabbed her shoulders.

"Is that who you want? Him?" His finger slipped beneath her panties, and she moaned as he stroked her slick folds. "Are you wet for him?"

"Please." She spread her legs wider, shifting her hips and rocking against his hand. "I need you."

"Me? Or him?" He grabbed her hair, pulling back her head. "Answer me."

"Patrick?" Her eyes widened. "Is this a game?"

"Answer me." His voice was rough as desire and anger waged war inside him.

She turned toward him, her lips red and pouty. "You. I'm wet for you."

He had to taste her. His mouth landed on hers, and she opened for him. He pushed her down on the bed, shoving up her dress and yanking off her underwear. He had to have her now, claim her as his in the most primal way. He pushed down his sweats, and she wrapped her legs around his hips.

"Fuck, you drive me crazy." He had to be inside her. He needed to show her that she wanted him. Just him. No one else. "Tell me you want me."

"Please, Patrick." She reached between them and grabbed his dick, rubbing it against her clit.

She was so slick and hot. He shifted and then thrust, sliding into her. She gasped as her body tightened around him.

"Look at me." He grabbed her chin. He wanted her to see that it was him bringing her this pleasure, not someone else. "Only I make you feel like this." His hips rocked, his dick sliding in and out, over and over.

Her eyes drifted partway closed, but she kept staring at him.

"Remember that." He lifted her legs, adjusting his angle as he thrust into her. When she moaned, he fucked her faster, hitting that spot again and again. "Do you think some twenty-something kid can do this? Make you feel like this?"

"Please.... Oh, yes.... Harder.... Please." Her words were half-moans as her body tightened under him, her hips rocking faster and faster.

He should slow the pace, make her suffer, make her beg for him, but the look of ecstasy on her face made his balls tighten. He needed her. He needed to feel her cling to him as she came. He pumped into her harder and faster. Her fingernails dug into his back as her breath came in hot pants in his ear. He moved his head, sucking on her breast and then biting down on her nipple.

"Patrick!" she screamed as her body tightened around his.

He groaned. She felt so fucking good. Perfect. His thrusts grew wild with need. The sound of flesh hitting flesh filled the room and then he stiffened as he came, emptying himself inside her and marking her as his.

CHAPTER 12: Annie

Annie's body was boneless. She adored Patrick. He could be a jerk sometimes, but what guy couldn't? She kissed his neck. "I love you."

His snore tickled her ear.

"Patrick." She shoved him. "Damn it, you fell asleep."

He often slept like the dead after sex, but he usually had the decency to roll off her first. She shoved him again, but it was like moving a boulder. A hot, naked.... Nope, they were both still dressed. She giggled. They'd been so hot for each other, but he was freaking heavy. She pushed again but nothing.

"Move. You're going to squish me." She slapped his back. "Wake up, you big jerk."

He grunted, nuzzling her neck.

God help her, a tingle started in her pussy. "No. Wake up." She pinched his side and then bit his earlobe.

"Ouch. Shit." He rolled off her. "Why'd you do that?" He rubbed his ear.

"You were squishing me." She sat up.

"You could've told me to move. You didn't have to bite me."

"You were sleeping."

"I was not." He sat up and took off his pants.

"Yes, you were." She stared at him. Something was wrong, but she couldn't quite remember what it was.

"What?" He pulled off his shirt and tossed it aside before dropping back onto the bed. He put his hands on the pillow behind his head and grinned up at her. "Come here, and you can have a closer look."

The pillow. Sophie's butt had been on that when.... "You're supposed to be on the couch."

The smile fled from his face. "I'm not sleeping on the sofa."

"Now, I remember." The entire night—at least the part before she'd gotten drunk—came flooding back. "We had a fight. You gave Vic—"

"I'm not apologizing for giving your brother money, and I'm not sleeping on the couch." He moved his arms from under his head and pulled up the blanket.

She got out of bed, letting her dress fall to her feet. His eyes darkened, and his face tightened with passion as she slowly removed her bra before dropping it.

"Come here."

His rough voice sent shivers through her body, and the growing bulge under the blankets told her exactly what they'd be doing if she obeyed. Her damn body chanted yes, yes, yes, but her pride was in charge now. "No."

"Annie, you have to understand about Vic."

He was talking to her in that lecturing tone all males seemed to use when women didn't do what they wanted. "I don't *have* to do anything, but that's not why I'm not getting in that bed with you."

"Then why?" His eyes narrowed, the desire fading from his gaze.

"Because I drive you fucking crazy, and you need your space. So, I'm giving it to you." She waved her hand between them. "This was a mistake."

"Right, because I'm not Dave," he mumbled as he punched his pillow and rolled to his side.

"Not Dave? What in the hell do you mean by that?" Now that she thought about it, he'd been muttering about Dave when they'd been having sex. At the time, she'd been too horny to care about anything but his touch.

"It's not that complicated."

"You're jealous of Dave?" She was dumbfounded. Patrick was sexy as sin, rich, successful, and a great guy. Dave was cute, poor, still finding his way professionally, and skinny. There was no competition.

"No." He rolled over, glaring at her. "I'm not, but if that's who you want, then...."

Her heart twisted. He couldn't be breaking up with her. She wanted to crawl onto the bed and use her body to persuade him that she was the one he wanted. Unfortunately, that only worked for the moment. She put on a T-shirt, covering her breasts from his dark gaze. She grabbed her pillow and blanket.

"Where are you going?"

"To sleep on the couch." She started for the door.

"Get in bed."

His tone demanded that she obey, but she'd grown up with alpha males. Commands like that guaranteed she'd do the opposite. She turned around, her chin jutting out. "I would, but I don't want to take up your precious space."

"Annie, stop being a"—he ran his hand across his face—"just get in bed. We both need some sleep."

"No." She stomped toward the door. He only wanted her in bed with him so he could hold her breast and sleep. He didn't want her, just her soft body. She stepped into the hallway, and a strong arm snaked around her waist. The damn man was quieter than a cat. She squeaked with surprise as he picked her up, tossing her over his shoulder. "Put me down."

"No." He strode toward their bed.

"We talked about this. You can't just pick me up and carry me around when you're pissed at me."

"Oh, I certainly can." He tossed her on the bed. "See."

"Fine. Then you shouldn't." She bounced once before sitting up.

"I haven't done it in ages."

"You shouldn't do it at all."

"I'll stop as soon as you stop being so stubborn." He dropped onto the bed.

"Me? You're the stubborn one." She tossed her legs over the side when his strong arm wrapped around her waist again, pulling her back against his chest "Let me go. I'm not having sex with you again."

"Tonight."

"What?" She twisted so she could see his face.

"Say the word tonight and we can sleep."

"What are you talking about?" She wiggled, trying to get free from his arms, but he tightened his grip. "Why do you want me to say tonight."

He sighed. "You're not having sex with me again tonight."

Oh." She stopped struggling. He wanted to have sex with her later, which proved his desire hadn't just been a heat of the moment kind of thing.

"Say it." His breath whispered against her ear. "I'm tired."

"You're always sleepy after sex." She relaxed in his arms.

"I know. So, say it, or I won't be able to sleep, and I'm tired." He yawned.

Her heart melted because this big, manly oaf needed her to sleep. That meant this wasn't over between them, right? She yawned. She was tipsy, satiated, and tired. Tonight, he wanted to hold her. Everything else could wait for tomorrow. "I'm not having sex with you again tonight." She wiggled her ass against his erection. "No matter how much I want to."

"Tease." He kissed her neck. "I'm willing to let you change your mind."

She laughed and then fell quiet for a moment, feeling his chest move against her back with each breath. "I never wanted Dave. We're just friends."

"You sure?" His arm tightened around her.

"Absolutely." She smiled. If he was jealous, he still cared for her.

"Is there someone else you do want?" The hint of anxiousness in his tone put her on edge.

"No." She could barely breathe. Did he want someone else? Did he want to swing or open their relationship?

"Good. I mean, if you do... If you want to...you know...."

"What?" She needed him to say it because she had no idea what he wanted.

"Try a threesome." He hesitated and then said, "I know a guy who'd be perfect for us."

"Oh. Okay." Her heart almost burst from her chest. Chelsea had been right. He wanted to try something else. Something he'd never mentioned. Something she'd never even considered.

"Just let me know. He...this guy...Lee is in town for the next week or so. Then he won't be back for a few months, maybe longer."

"You've thought about this?" She was shocked.

"Some."

It sounded like he had it all planned. "And this is something...you want to do?" Her voice was barely a whisper. She'd been with guys before him, but she'd always been a one woman-one guy kind of gal.

"If you do." He kissed her neck.

She froze in his arms. She couldn't believe that he actually wanted another person in their bed. He'd told her before that he wasn't into threesomes.

"If you don't want to, that's okay." His voice was tense and his body stiff behind her.

Did she? Not really but she couldn't deny that she was getting wet at the thought of Patrick and another man, worshiping her body, demanding her to please them while they pleased her. It wasn't like he wanted to bring another woman into their bed. Her mind screeched to a halt. "Would you and him...?"

"We'd do whatever you wanted us to do."

"Together? You and him...you know."

This time when he stiffened it was everywhere except his cock. The hardness there disappeared. "No. I'm not bi, and neither is Lee."

"Oh. Good." She was able to breathe again. She didn't want to see him with another woman, but she really didn't want to see him with another man.

"So do you want to meet him?" His tone was flat.

"Yeah, I guess." She'd do this for him and maybe just a little for herself but mainly for him.

CHAPTER 13: Patrick

Patrick downed his second cup of coffee as he stared at his phone. His stomach twisted like it was going to revolt, but not just because of the copious quantity of alcohol he'd had last night but because of the text.

UNKNOWN: It's Lee. Ethan said you wanted to talk to me. How about lunch?

He needed to answer, but what was he going to do? No, he knew what he was going to do. He just didn't want to do it.

PATRICK: Okay. Two o'clock?

That gave him an hour. Hopefully, Lee was busy. The guy had texted him at ten that morning.

LEE: Sure. The Club?

Fuck. He ran his hand through his hair. He had no way to go but forward.

PATRICK: Yeah.

They may as well meet there. The food was excellent, and they wouldn't have to worry about offending anyone when he asked Lee to fuck his girlfriend. His jaw clenched so hard he thought his teeth were going to shatter.

"Hey." Annie walked into the kitchen. Her hair was a mess, and the makeup from last night was smeared under her eyes. She had on a pair of her tiny fuck-me shorts that he drooled over and a baggy T-shirt.

He wanted nothing more than to push her against the counter and fuck her right there. He should bring her to the edge and stop when she was so close to coming that she'd do anything for release. Then he'd get her to agree to never, ever have a threesome.

She poured some coffee. "Want a refill?" She held up the pot.

"No. I'm fine with what I have. As a matter of fact, this is enough for me. More than enough. More than I'd ever dreamed, but you.... Go ahead and drink your fucking coffee." He stood and stormed out of the room.

"What the hell was that about?" Annie followed him into the living room.

He grabbed his keys and then remembered that he'd left his car at the Club. Shit-fuck. Today was going to be one of the worst days of his life. He turned to face her. "I need a ride." God, it killed him to ask, but it was that or call an Uber.

"Where's your car?"

"The Club."

"I knew you went there last night." Her pretty face pinched with anger.

"Of course, I went there, but I went to talk to my friends. I didn't spend the night bumping and grinding all over other women."

"Yes, I danced, but I did not bump and grind on anyone."

"Please. I've danced with you. You do more grinding than a construction site."

Her breath hitched. "Fuck you."

"You already did. You came home all hot and horny after rubbing your stuff all over other men. I just happened to be the lucky dick around."

"Go to hell." She walked into their bedroom, slamming the door behind her.

"Fuck me." He tapped his stupid, thick skull against the wall. This was not how he'd wanted to start the day.

CHAPTER 14: Patrick

Patrick sat at the bar in the Club's restaurant waiting for Lee. He'd arrived forty minutes early, and that was about thirty minutes ago, but staying in the house with Annie had not been a good idea. Right now, he'd probably ruin their relationship just so he didn't have to go through with this.

"Hey." Lee pulled out a chair and sat next to him. "A beer and a shot of bourbon"—he said to the bartender before pointing to Patrick's glass—"and another for my friend."

"Thanks." He tried to look at the guy, but he just couldn't. This man was going to see Annie naked. Touch her breasts, kiss them, lick her pussy, and fuck her. He wanted to grab his glass and smash it over Lee's head.

The bartender put their drinks down in front of them.

"Put it on my tab." Lee tossed back his shot. "Are you, okay?"

"Yeah." He was as far from okay as he could be.

"You sure? You look like your dog just died."

"My dogs are fine." Shit, if they broke up what would they do with the dogs? He didn't want to lose them too.

"I didn't even know you had dogs." Lee laughed. "Bad day? Or really good time last night?"

"Why are you asking about my night?" He hadn't realized that the guy was such a jerk. This wouldn't work at all.

"Because you're drinking club soda."

"So." Patrick turned to him, and his heart, which already weighed two tons, got heavier. He'd kind of forgotten how attractive the other man was. Annie was going to love Lee. He had sandy blonde hair, blue eyes as clear as the sky, and some crinkles around them. Women fucking loved those.

"Did you want to talk some other time?" Lee watched him curiously.

"No. Let's get a table toward the back." Not that anything stayed a secret at the Club. Soon, everyone would know that he had shared Annie with Lee. Some of the others would want to be next.

"Okay." Lee grabbed his beer and headed for the other side of the restaurant.

Patrick followed. She was probably going to like his ass too, and his body. Lee was leaner than Patrick, not as muscular but not skinny. The man was tall and slender with lean, defined muscles. "Fuck."

"Did you say something?" Lee glanced over his shoulder.

"No." He sat at a table. "I just want to get this over with," he mumbled under his breath.

Lee took the seat across from him. A waiter brought them menus, and they both looked them over in silence. Lee put his down and waited. Patrick pretended that he was having a hard time deciding what to order, but he was actually buying himself time before he sealed his fate and ruined his relationship. Ruined? Ha. His relationship had already gone sour. This was supposed to fix it.

"Do you need more time?" asked the waiter when he stopped at their table.

"No. I'll have the burger and fries." He handed the waiter his menu.

"The chef salad," said Lee.

"And...." He stopped the waiter. "Bring me a double whiskey. Straight."

The waiter nodded and left.

"A little hair of the dog, huh?" Lee smirked. "I've been there before."

"Yeah. I guess." His stomach and head didn't want to be in the same room with alcohol, but he'd never be able to have this conversation without it.

"So, what's up?" Lee sipped his beer.

"Let's talk after we eat." That way he could pound a few shots too. "How's the oil business going?"

"Small talk it is." Lee shrugged as he finished his beer.

Patrick downed another shot, pushing his barely touched plate away. "I never would've guessed you for a salad man. You're from Texas for God's sake."

"Texans have heart attacks too." Lee dropped his napkin in the empty salad bowl "Don't get me wrong, I love a good T-bone but not on a daily basis." He grinned. "I love life more than a steak."

"Yeah." He stared at his burger. "Annie would have my head for ordering a burger and fries."

"Annie?"

Here it was—the perfect opportunity. "My girlfriend."

"Congratulations." Lee held up his beer to toast.

"Thanks." Patrick lifted his water when he realized his shot glass was empty.

"Serious?"

"I think so."

"Oh." Lee winced.

"No. We're good. She's great." At least the last part was true.

"I'm glad. My momma has been dropping hints that it's time I settle down, but I've been ignoring her." Lee's lips tipped upward in a half-smile. "I'm not ready for a one-woman only life." His eyes drifted across the room as if searching for someone.

"That's what I wanted to talk to you about." He waved the waiter over. He tapped his shot glass. "Another and.... Actually, just bring the bottle."

"Yes, sir. And for you?" The waiter turned to Lee.

"Water." Lee's focus was now completely on Patrick. "I think I'm gonna need a clear head for this conversation."

"Unlike me." Patrick snorted. "I need to be drunker than I am right now."

"And I wish I hadn't had that last shot." Lee tipped the empty shot glass in front of him upside down.

"Nah, this conversation should be easy for you." Any man would be happy to fuck Annie. He grabbed his phone and flipped through the pictures until he found his favorite one of her. They'd been on their way to meet his family. She'd been nervous and so damn cute. She'd worn a peach sundress that'd highlighted her smooth tan skin. She'd left her hair loose and had worn barely any makeup. She was so beautiful, and he'd been so happy because he'd thought she'd been his. "This is Annie."

Lee took the phone and whistled. "Nice. Does she have a sister?"

The waiter brought the drinks and Patrick filled his glass tossing it back before taking the phone from Lee. "Nope, just brothers."

"Too bad." Lee lifted his glass of water.

"Not really. You don't need her to have a sister. You can have her." He would've sworn that his heart would explode over something like that, but instead it'd folded in on itself and had died.

"Excuse me?" Lee almost choked on his drink.

He closed his eyes for a moment. He had to do this. Lee was a good guy. He was too attractive for Patrick's liking, but the man wasn't around too much so he was the perfect candidate. He inhaled deeply and opened his eyes, staring right at Lee. "She wants a threesome. You interested?"

"Wow." Lee turned his shot glass right-side up, grabbed the bottle of whiskey, and poured himself a shot. He tossed it back before pouring another one. "I hadn't expected that."

"What did you think I wanted?"

"I wasn't sure. Money. A favor." Lee's lips quirked up in a lopsided grin. "I guess it is kind of a favor but not one I would've guessed in a million years." He picked up the glass and hesitated, his hand halfway to his mouth. "I thought threesomes weren't your thing?"

"They aren't." He'd never enjoyed them. The sex was sex, and an orgasm was always pleasurable, but he'd never liked the group thing.

"Then why?"

"She wants to try it."

"Tell her you don't." Lee drank his shot.

If only it were that simple. "We've done a lot together." He shrugged. "She's tried everything I've asked."

"Ah. You feel you owe her." Lee nodded.

"Kind of. I guess." He didn't want to lose her, and this was becoming a big wedge in their relationship.

"So that's why you picked me. I'm a one-time thing."

"That *was* one of Ethan's selling points." He grinned a little.

"Ethan?"

"He suggested I talk to you."

"Now that you mention it, I do see his hand in this."

"What do you mean by that?" He and Ethan had been friends since the Marines. He trusted the man with is life.

"Nothing, except he doesn't understand relationships."

"And you do?"

"Yep."

Lee didn't elaborate, and Patrick didn't ask. Even though Lee's mom was pushing for a wedding, the other man could've been married six times already for all he knew.

"And you don't think this is a good idea?" He certainly didn't, but he'd do anything for Annie.

"Not if you have to get plastered to talk about it." Lee poured himself another shot. "If a couple wants to try a threesome or likes to invite others into their bed, I say go for it, but if one of them doesn't want to do it then they shouldn't."

"I get that. I do." But then he'd lose her, not today or tomorrow but eventually.

"Did you ever make her do something she didn't want to do?"

"No. Of course not." He'd never do something like that.

"Well?" Lee looked at him like he was an idiot.

"It's not that simple. I've tried threesomes. She hasn't. I think that if we do it this one time, that'll be it. Her curiosity will be satisfied." He prayed that was how it'd work.

"I should be insulted." Lee grinned.

"Come on." He wasn't in the mood for jokes. "Will you do it?" He wanted to puke or punch something because he hated asking this guy to fuck his girlfriend—the woman he loved.

"Do you really think you'll be okay with this?" Lee's blue eyes were serious.

"Yeah. I told you. I've done them before."

"With a woman you cared about?"

"Yeah. I didn't love it, but I lived." He hadn't loved her either.

"Did the relationship?"

"No. I wouldn't be in this one if it had, but it didn't end because of the threesome. She moved." It'd been over before that, though. She'd wanted to go to more and more swinger parties, and he hadn't.

"Okay." Lee drank his shot.

"You'll do it?"

"On one condition."

"What?" Right now, he'd promise just about anything because he couldn't have this conversation with another guy. He just couldn't.

"I get to meet her first."

"Of course. We'll meet for drinks before we start."

"No. I mean, I get to meet her alone."

"Why?" He didn't like this at all.

"I want to make sure she's okay with it too."

"She's the one who wants to do it."

"Is she a sub? I know you weren't a Dom, but things change."

"No. I'm not a Dom, and she's definitely not a sub." She was the least sub-like woman he knew except actual Dommes.

"Then she may want to have a threesome, but she may not want to have it with me."

"Good point." He shrugged. "Fine. You can meet her, but no touching, kissing, or anything else unless I'm there."

"Deal." Lee paused for a second and then shook his head. "Let me just say this one more time, I think you're making a mistake."

"I hope not." If he was, they'd break up, but they were on the verge of that anyway. This was his only chance to keep them together.

CHAPTER 15: Annie

Annie stood in the kitchen, cutting up vegetables for a grilled vegetarian enchilada she was perfecting for a quinceañera she was catering later this month.

The dogs barked and ran into the living room.

"He's home." She sliced a yellow pepper, hitting the cutting board a little harder than necessary. "He's such a frigging jerk-wad," she muttered to herself. "He asks me to sleep with another man and then has the audacity to get mad because I danced with someone besides him. What an idiot."

"Hey." Patrick stopped in the kitchen doorway. "Smells good."

"Thanks." She kept her eyes on the veggies even though his rich, deep voice made her body tingle. She refused to acknowledge that he sounded sad and a little worried. If she looked at him, she knew her resolve would melt, and she'd forgive him too easily.

"Want some wine?" He walked to the fridge, carrying a brown bag.

"No." After last night, she didn't even want to look at alcohol.

"You sure?" He pulled out a bottle of zinfandel and a bottle of whiskey. He tossed a couple of cubes of ice into a glass and poured himself a drink.

"Positive." Apparently, he was ready to get drunk again tonight. It wasn't like him to drink this much. She glanced at him for a second.

He put the wine in the refrigerator before walking across the kitchen and stopping behind her. She struggled to focus. The man didn't even need to touch her to make her knees weak. Just the heat of his body and how he towered over her, smelling so damn sexy, made her melt. She was such a lovesick fool when it came to him.

"How much longer before you're done?" He still didn't touch her, but he leaned a little closer, watching over her shoulder.

"Are you that hungry?" She wasn't going to let him charm his way out of trouble this time.

"No, but I...I'd like to talk to you about something."

"Did you change your mind about loaning Vic the money?" Her knife froze on the cutting board.

"No." His voice hardened. "And I'm not going to."

"Then what do you want to talk about?" Her temper sparked to life. They needed to get this...whatever this was between them out in the open. The enchiladas could wait or rot for all she cared. She put the knife down and walked to the sink, her legs feeling like they weighed eight hundred pounds each as she prayed that this wasn't going to be the end of them.

"You don't have to stop. We can talk when you're done."

"I'm done. Believe me. I'm done." She washed her hands and pulled the wine from the fridge.

"I thought you didn't—"

"I changed my mind." She filled her glass to the top, forcing herself to take a big chug. Her stomach twisted, but it was already turned inside out along with her heart. She leaned against the counter. "So, I'm waiting. Talk."

"Let's go to the living room." He started for the door.

Her eyes dropped to his jeans which hugged his perfectly bitable, kissable ass. She could not let her mind wander there because mad or not, she'd jump the man, and she wasn't going to make this easy on him. "Here is fine."

"Okay." He stopped in the doorway. "But I think it'd be better if we were both sitting." He smiled shyly. "I'd feel better sitting."

"How you feel isn't my concern right now."

"Oh. Wow." His eyes widened. "Where the fuck did that come from?"

"You're kidding, right?" She had no idea what he was thinking. He was essentially helping her brother right back into addiction, and he'd accused her of grinding on other men.

"If it's about this morning, I'm sorry. I shouldn't have said anything but.... Damn it, Annie, I didn't like not knowing where you were and then when you showed up in that fuck-me dress with Dave—"

"It was not a fuck-me dress, and what I wear when I go out is none of your business."

"It is so my business." He strode over to her. "You are my girlfriend and—"

"That doesn't mean you can tell me what to wear." She shoved at his chest.

"I don't fucking tell you what to wear, and I'm never going to, but you can't stop me from being jealous." He grabbed her hand and kissed her palm. "I love you like crazy, Annie Argotos."

"Damn you." She swayed toward him, her heart morphing into a big lump of gooey feelings. "I should stay angry with you for at least the evening."

"Please don't be mad at me." He kissed her softly. "Everything I do is for you."

"That's a lovely lie, Patrick," she said against his lips, not willing to break the contact.

"But it's not a lie." His hand slid around her waist to her ass, pulling her closer.

His growing erection pressed against her and damn him, she wanted this. Him. She ran her tongue across his lower lip, and he moaned.

"Annie, you drive me mad." He lifted her.

"The feeling is mutual." She wrapped her legs around his hips and her arms around his neck. "Now, unzip those pants and fuck me."

His eyes flared green fire as he pushed her against the wall, tugging her legs from his waist and shoving down her shorts. She fell into his kiss as his mouth devoured hers. His hands were everywhere, squeezing her breasts, stroking her stomach and then sliding between her legs.

"Oh...yes, Patrick." She clung to him as his fingers teased her slick folds. The best kind of desire raced through her—lust mixed with love.

"Put your hands on my shoulders." He unzipped his pants and grabbed her waist, lifting her until her toes barely touched the floor.

She obeyed without hesitation. She wanted this as much as he did. He pressed against her, holding her up with his hard body, as he lifted one of her legs, bending her knee and opening her wide for him. He grabbed his dick, sliding it along her pussy, his hot tip prodding at her opening.

"Yes. Please." She wiggled her hips the best she could to try and take him inside.

"Fuck." He shoved into her in one hard push and then his mouth was on hers, his tongue thrusting into her as his hot cock filled her.

Her fingers dug into his shoulder as his lips found her neck, kissing and nipping as he pumped into her faster and harder.

"Yes, oh God." She clung to him, trying to keep that thick, hard dick inside her, pressing against the spot that seemed to be made just for him. That place only he could find. She moaned as he retreated, but then he was back, fucking her faster and faster. With her leg held open he filled her with each thrust. Pleasure roared through her as his hot breath teased her ear, and his body took hers. She screamed, her pussy tightening around him, pulling him deeper—into her body, her heart, and her soul.

"Fuck...Annie." He stiffened, moaning against her neck as he came.

"Next time, I want you naked." She hung loose in his arms, one hand tangled in his hair as the other skimmed over his shoulders and the soft fabric of his shirt.

"Deal." He smiled against her neck.

"That tickles." She wiggled.

He kissed the side of her face before letting her leg drop, but he kept her pressed between him and the wall. He cupped her cheeks, staring into her eyes. "I love you, Annie. Nothing is going to change that."

"I love you too." She didn't like the concern on his face and in his voice.

"We still need to talk."

"Right." Her mind tumbled over what he needed to talk to her about.

"I'll grab the drinks." He took a step back, zipping up his pants.

"I'll get dressed."

"You don't have to." His eyes were dark and hooded as he stared at the juncture between her legs.

She had no problem sitting around without pants. They always found something fun to do sans clothing, but if this conversation was that serious, she didn't want to be semi-dressed. "I think I should put on my shorts." She grabbed her underwear and stepped into them.

"I think you should always be naked."

"Really?" She gave him a smug look. "Even when I go to work or go out clubbing with my friends?"

"No." His face hardened. "You should always be naked at home. With me."

"Depending on how this conversation goes, you may get to undress me again." She pulled on her shorts.

The desire fled from his face, replaced by an emotion she didn't quite catch before he turned toward the counter. Had it been uncertainty? Sadness? He grabbed their drinks and walked into the living room.

She followed, her stomach dropping to her toes. He was arrogant, cocky, and sweet, but he was never nervous around her. She took her glass as she sat next to him.

He stared into his whiskey, not saying a word.

"Patrick, please. You're making me nervous." She took a big gulp of her drink.

"I met with Lee this afternoon."

"Lee?" That name was familiar, but she didn't know why.

"Yeah. Lee." He stared at her, his eyes searching hers. "He wants to meet you."

"Me?" She pointed at herself. "Who is Lee, and why does he want to meet me?"

He glanced away. "He agreed to...with us, but he wants to meet you first."

"Oh. Okay." This man that Patrick wanted her to have sex with wanted to meet her. It made sense. The guy probably needed to make sure he found her attractive. It wouldn't do for him not to be able to perform. She almost laughed.

"I told him I had to check with you first, but you'd probably be able to meet him for dinner tonight."

"Tonight?" Her throat almost closed on the word.

"If you don't want to—"

"Tonight is fine." She didn't want to meet this guy at all. She wasn't even sure she wanted the three of them to do this. Part of her purred at the idea of two guys kissing her, touching her, filling her one after the other, but another part froze in fear. She had no idea where her and Patrick's relationship went after something like this.

"Okay. I can drop you off at the Club—"

"Drop me off? You're not going with me?" She needed him there with her.

"He wants to meet with you alone."

"No." She shook her head. "I want you there. I don't even know this guy."

"He won't agree to the threesome unless he meets with you by yourself."

"That isn't a threesome. That's just him and me and I'm not having sex with—"

"What? No. This is just dinner. No sex." His eyes darkened, and he grabbed her chin. "I mean it. No sex tonight."

She should be furious that he was giving her orders on what she could and couldn't do, but she was too relieved that he didn't expect her to sleep with this guy. "Okay. Good. Because I want you to be there when we…. You know." The only way she'd make it through this was if he was there with her.

CHAPTER 16: Patrick

Patrick got out of the Uber in the parking lot of La Petite Mort Club. He offered his hand to Annie. Hers was small and cold in his. She was nervous. Good. Maybe she'd decide that a threesome wasn't worth all this anxiety. "Ready?"

She tugged down her short dress, and her boobs almost popped from the top. This was the first time in his life he'd ever frowned at cleavage. It took everything he had not to snap at her for wearing the sexiest dress she owned.

"Do I look okay?" She peered up at him.

His annoyance disappeared as soon as he saw the worry in her big brown eyes. "You're beautiful." He pulled her close, never wanting to let her go. He should beg her to get back into the car so they could go home—just the two of them, but she'd never had a threesome. If she wanted to try it, he'd do it for her. He'd do anything for her. He kissed her softly. "Don't worry. It's just dinner." That was damn well all it was going to be. He'd be upstairs with Ethan, watching every course.

"I know. I just never met someone that I'd already agreed to…. You know. It's weird."

"It is." *Please let her change her mind. Please. Please.*

"I don't know how Sarah managed to go through with it."

"Her situation was different."

"Yeah, she hadn't agreed to have sex with anyone, but she had to stand in that room while you all watched." She shivered.

"Is that a good shiver or a bad one? You can change your mind and do a Viewing instead." He wouldn't love sitting there and watching guys leer at her and ask her to show her tits, but it'd be a lot better than what was going to happen. Lee would do a lot more than look.

"No. I'd never want to do a Viewing. All those men staring at me when I can't even see them." She shivered again. "No, thanks."

"If you're sure." He smiled slightly when he really wanted to throttle her. Yeah, guys staring was so much worse than a stranger fucking her.

"I'm sure." She took his arm. "We should probably go inside. We're already late."

"He'll wait." He pulled her into his arms and kissed her with all the love and passion he had, silently begging her to change her mind, to decide that he was enough for her.

He'd never been enough for any of the women in his past. Everyone he'd ever cared about had eventually cheated on him. He'd thought Annie was different, and she was. She wasn't cheating. She wanted to try something new, and she wanted him there with her. He wasn't sure which was worse.

"Patrick." She moaned against his mouth as her arms wrapped around his neck, her lush body pushing against his.

He cupped her ass, pulling her closer. He should fuck her right here in the garage. He could lay her on a car or push her against the wall. No matter how charming Lee was with his Texas drawl, she'd be thinking of him with her thighs wet and her panties gone.

She broke the kiss. Touching his face, her eyes searching his. "Are you okay?"

"Yeah." He wasn't, not at all, but she wanted this. He couldn't ruin it for her. He loved her too much. He forced himself to smirk. "I want you wet and eager, thinking of me when you meet him."

"I'm always thinking of you." She kissed him softly.

His heart twisted because she wouldn't be when Lee was eating her out or fucking her. He didn't care how much she loved him. She'd be focused on the man bringing her pleasure. With an inexperienced guy, she might have been able to close her eyes and imagine someone else, but that didn't happen at the Club. The men here—him, Lee, and the others—knew how to keep a woman in the present when they fucked her. Maybe he should've gone with some guy off the street.

CHAPTER 17: Annie

Annie clung to Patrick's hand as he led her into the restaurant to a table in the back. A well-dressed, drop-dead gorgeous man stood. The guy was tall, lean but muscular with golden hair, and a ruggedly handsome face.

"Patrick." The man nodded, extending his arm.

The two shook hands and then Patrick turned toward her. "Lee, this is Annie."

Patrick's voice sounded normal. The damn man wasn't even a little nervous, but why would he be? He wasn't going to let this guy do things to *his* body.

"Pleasure, ma'am." Lee's blue eyes sparkled as he held out his hand.

If she hadn't been watching closely, she wouldn't have seen the quick dip his gaze took down her frame and the extra second or so that he paused on her breasts. Usually, she loved the sneaky ogle that gentlemen gave her boobs, but tonight she wanted to cover them up. She would've worn a parka if she didn't think it'd upset Patrick. He wanted to do this. She'd enjoyed everything they'd tried so far; she had to trust that she'd enjoy this too.

"Hi." Her eyes skimmed over the other man as she took his hand. His grip was warm and strong without being forceful. She loved Patrick and Lee was beyond attractive. She was pretty sure that nervous or not, she'd enjoy the threesome. She just wasn't sure how she'd feel about it later.

"Would you like some wine?" Lee held out a chair.

"Yes, thank you." She sat, picking up the napkin and then putting it down. She wasn't sure where to look or what to do. *Get a grip*. She'd just think of this as a first date. *Yeah, one where she'd already agreed to give over the goods*. No, that didn't matter. She could change her mind. Nothing was signed in blood.

He poured some wine into her glass and turned toward Patrick. "Why don't we meet in the Club in a few hours?"

"Sounds good." Patrick didn't move.

Lee grinned slightly as he sat. His gaze went to Annie. "What do you do for a living?"

She glanced at Patrick. Was he changing his mind? *Please, make him sit and tell this man that the threesome was off.*

He bent and kissed her. She expected a quick peck on the lips, but his hand captured the back of her neck, holding her in place as his tongue slipped between her lips. His mouth was rough, devouring, claiming her as his. Everything but him disappeared as her fingers clasped his shirt, and she got lost in his kiss. His hand tightened almost painfully in her hair, and she clutched the chair, trying to steady her world.

He pulled away; his eyes locked with hers. "I'll see you in an hour."

She nodded because the damn man had stolen her words and her thoughts.

He turned and strode away.

"As I was saying...." Lee grinned as he watched Patrick's retreating form for a second before looking back at her. "What do you do for a living?"

"Ah...." She stared after Patrick. He was never this possessive. Thank God that this was the restaurant at the Club because no one paid any attention to that incendiary kiss.

"Are you okay?" asked Lee.

The waiter came over. "Are you ready to order?"

"Yes." Annie picked up her menu. She wanted to be done with this dinner...with this entire evening.

"I need a few minutes," said Lee.

"Yes, sir." The waiter walked away.

"Annie, are you sure about this?" He studied her.

"About dinner? Yeah. I usually get the—"

"I'm not talking about dinner."

"Oh." Her chest froze like she'd inhaled icy air.

"Darlin', take a deep breath."

She did and her moment of panic subsided. "Sorry."

"No reason for apologies." His blue eyes had darkened a bit with concern. "But I want the truth."

"About what?"

"Are you sure about this?"

"Oh." She couldn't mess this up. Patrick had never asked her to do something that she hadn't enjoyed. "Yeah." She smiled again but this time it was wider and more friendly. "Absolutely." She grabbed her glass and took a gulp.

"Then"—his eyes raked over her body—"let's get on with it."

"What?" She choked, trying not to spit her wine all over his handsome face.

"You're ready. He's ready." Lee leaned back, his gaze hot and heavy on her chest before lifting to her face. "I'm more than ready. You're a very attractive woman. Patrick's a lucky man."

"Well...uhm...thank you." She gulped down the rest of her drink.

"Are you sure you're fine with this?" He picked up the wine bottle, and she let him fill her glass. "I've had my share of threesomes, and you don't act like a woman who's...eager for the scene to happen."

"I am. Really. It's good. Patrick wants this—"

"Patrick wants this?" He seemed surprised.

"I do too, of course. He isn't making me do this or anything. He's not like that." She didn't want anyone to think she was being forced. Patrick would never do that. Ever.

"But this was his idea." His tone was halfway between a statement and a question.

"Yeah." She wanted to yell, of course it was his idea. She loved watching threesomes and foursomes, but she'd never thought about participating. Patrick was more than enough. Her heart twisted because she obviously wasn't enough for him.

"I see." He leaned back against his chair, frowning.

She'd blown it. Her face heated. Those were the exact wrong words. She imagined being on her knees in front of this guy while Patrick frowned down at her, except he wouldn't be frowning because he wanted to see her suck another guy's dick. Why? Why would he want to see that?

"I think you and Patrick should talk about this. Really talk."

"No. Please." She leaned forward.

His eyes dropped to her cleavage before jumping quickly back to her face.

"I do want to do this." She took his hand. "I'm just nervous. I don't know you, and I've never had a threesome, and it's just.... I've seen them a lot of times but participating...with my boyfriend just seems...."

"Weird?"

She nodded and then grabbed her glass, chugging every last drop of wine in it. She would've tapped the bottom if she'd thought it'd make a difference.

"Whoa, slow down." He touched her arm. "You haven't even eaten."

"Suddenly, I'm not hungry." She couldn't eat, not thinking about what she was going to do with this guy.

"You should." He lifted his hand to wave at the waiter.

"Wait."

He dropped his arm, his gaze going back to her.

"When? When did you...? When were we...?"

He frowned at her.

"Oh shit, I'm sorry. I thought...." She was so embarrassed. He'd said that they should get on with it, but he'd never actually agreed to do it. "I understand if you don't want to. I shouldn't have assumed that—"

"Stop. Okay." He took her hand. "I definitely want to help the two of you out. I've known Patrick for years, and he's a good guy."

"He is." Her entire body warmed at the thought of him. He was kind, considerate, sexy as hell, and she'd do anything not to lose him. "He's the best."

"How about we all sit and talk. Get to know each other together."

"Now?" This was going to happen now. Her hand trembled under his.

"We can just talk."

"No. I'd rather get this over with." She grimaced. "I'm sorry. That didn't come out right."

He laughed. "I think it came out perfectly, and you're right." He stood, offering her his hand. "Let's go."

"What about Patrick?"

"I'm sure he's already on his way." He nodded at one of the cameras in the restaurant.

CHAPTER 18: Patrick

Patrick stopped by Annie's side. She was at the bar alone. "Where's Lee?" Their meeting had been short. Very short. She'd guzzled some wine and then they'd left—no dinner and almost no talking. "Did you change your mind?" The breath caught in his chest, hanging on hope.

"No." She shook her head and waved at the bartender. "Actually, we're going to do it now."

"Now?" Fuck, he wasn't ready for this.

"Yeah." She smiled, but there was nervousness in her eyes. "Unless you don't want to."

"What? Of course, I want to. I just didn't think we'd do it tonight."

"Do you want to wait?"

"Uh.... No. This is perfect. I wasn't sure how it'd gone since you skipped dinner, but I guess it went great. I'm thrilled." He wanted to puke.

"More wine, Annie?" asked Bea, the bartender.

"Yes, please."

"And give me a double whiskey," he said.

"Got it." Bea walked away to grab the drinks.

Patrick sat next to Annie, regretting that he hadn't ordered the entire bottle. He was going to need it. Fear, nervousness, and dread raged through him. It was like a mission all over again, except this time there was no latent excitement of challenging himself to outsmart the bad guys. It was just a risky mission with no reward. He couldn't believe they were actually going to do this. "Where's Lee?" he asked again.

"He went to talk to someone to ah...arrange things."

"Good." It was and it wasn't. Someone had to get a playroom, and he didn't think he'd be able to force himself to say the words. He had no idea how he was going to get through the next hour or so. Hell, his dick wasn't even excited. It was literally down in the dumps.

"Yeah. Good." She accepted her glass from the bartender and drank half.

He downed his shot and pushed his glass forward for a refill.

"Hey." Lee slapped his back as he came up to them. "Glad you could make it."

"Wouldn't miss it." He tried to smile, but he was pretty sure all he did was bare his teeth at the other man.

"I can see that." Lee's tone was a mix of sarcasm and humor.

"You want a drink?" Maybe if he delayed long enough, they could all go home without doing this.

"Yeah, but not here. I had some bottles delivered to a private playroom." Lee's eyes skimmed over Annie's breasts, and Patrick wanted to punch him. "I thought we might want some privacy for the first time."

"First?" Annie almost choked on her wine. "I thought you lived in Texas."

"I do." Lee skimmed his fingers across the skin on her arm. "But I usually come to town a few times a year. I've been visiting more lately and maybe I'll make a few extra trips just to see you."

That was fucking fantastic. It was exactly what he didn't want. Patrick grabbed the side of his chair to keep himself from tossing Annie over his shoulder and getting them both out of here.

"Oh." She smiled. "As long as that's okay with Patrick."

It was not okay with him. None of this was okay with him, but she'd shivered when Lee had touched her. She wanted this, and he was being a selfish jerk. Still, he couldn't force himself to agree to more than this one time. "Let's see how tonight goes."

"An excellent idea," said Lee. "But I do have one condition."

He wasn't in the mood for conditions unless he could use it to end this entire charade. "What?"

"Tonight, you follow my lead." Lee's eyes locked with his.

"What exactly does that mean?" He wasn't going to let this get out of control.

"Don't worry. I'll make sure that nothing and I mean *nothing* is done in that room unless all three of us want to do it."

If that were really the case, then this night would be over before it began.

Lee turned toward Annie. "Is this okay with you?"

"Ah...Patrick?" Her big brown eyes pleaded with him.

"Yeah." He fucking hated himself for agreeing, but he couldn't refuse her. "Except my condition is that she's really in charge. She has the final say."

"Yes, sir." Lee rubbed his hands together. "We're gonna have some fun tonight." He held out his arm to Annie.

Her dark eyes met Patrick's, and he nodded. She had to get used to the guy's touch, even if it killed him.

CHAPTER 19: Annie

Annie almost jumped when Patrick closed the door behind them. Usually, she and Patrick observed and had their fun in the rooms above the playrooms. They'd been in a few of the playrooms before, but it had always been just the two of them. Alone. Together.

"Patrick, why don't you pour us some drinks?" Lee led her to the couch.

At least he hadn't taken her right to the giant bed that sat in the center of the room. In the center? Hell, it took up almost the entire room. "How many people fit on that thing?" she mumbled, unable to pull her eyes away from the mattress.

"A lot." Lee laughed as he sat, pulling her down to the couch.

Patrick walked over to them and handed her a glass of wine.

"Thanks." She took a big sip, her mouth dry from nervousness.

"Relax, sugar." Lee kissed the back of her hand. "We won't bite. Unless you want us to." His eyes sparkled as his tongue darted out, flicking her knuckles.

She gasped, and her gaze jumped to Patrick. He stared down at her, his expression unreadable.

"Scootch over, darlin'. Make some room for your boyfriend." Lee dropped her hand, patting the couch on his side. "Where's my drink?" He glanced up at Patrick.

He grunted something and walked back to the bar in the corner.

Lee leaned closer to her, his hot breath tickling her ear. "Trust me, sugar. Everything is going to be okay. I promise."

She couldn't move. This wasn't really happening. She should stop this. Patrick's eyes met hers as he strode back to the couch. She silently pleaded with him to sit next to her. He handed Lee his drink and then sat on her other side.

"Your girl's a little nervous. Maybe you should help her relax."

"Good idea." Patrick's warm hands touched her shoulders, turning her so her back was to him.

His fingers massaged her neck, and she relaxed. This she liked. This she wanted—him.

"Go ahead, sugar. Lean against him. Feel his heat."

She did, soaking in the warmth of his strong chest as his hands worked their magic on her shoulders and neck.

"Drink up, now." Lee took a sip of his drink.

She did too, watching as his tongue darted out, cleaning the smidge of bourbon from his mouth. She couldn't help it. Her tongue slid across her lips too.

"That's it, sugar." Lee leaned back against the couch, stretching out his legs.

Her eyes dropped to his lap as Patrick kissed her neck. Lee was definitely aroused, and he wasn't a small man. Her gazed skimmed slowly back up his body.

"Give me your feet." Lee's blue eyes had grown darker with passion, and he had a sexy smirk on his lips.

Patrick's fingers stilled on her neck.

"Patrick?" She turned her head. His face was like granite.

"I'll help." Lee bent, grabbing one of her legs and stretching it out on the couch. "This is getting in the way." He tossed her shoe aside, and his strong fingers began massaging her foot.

She moaned. She couldn't help it. She was on her feet all day at work, and this felt freaking fantastic.

"Fuck." Patrick's mouth captured hers, and this wasn't a teasing, coaxing kiss; it was pure passion and need. He devoured her, one hand wrapping in her hair to hold her still for his kiss while the other cupped her breast.

Her back arched, pushing into his touch as she reached over her head and wrapped her arms around his neck. His hand slid inside her dress, squeezing the soft flesh as the other one wrapped around her waist, yanking her backward, closer to him. Lee's hand fell away from her foot, but she didn't care. All she felt was Patrick—his need, his desire. His lips traveled to her throat, kissing his way down her shoulder.

"Unzip her dress." Lee's husky voice made her start. For a second, she'd forgotten that he was there.

Patrick must've too because he stilled for a moment. "Annie?" He kissed her quickly. It was a question, a seeking of permission.

She touched his cheek. Even after she'd agreed he still wanted to make sure. She couldn't deny him anything. "I love you."

"I love you too." He kissed her again. His fingers hesitating on her zipper before his hand dropped away. "You do it." He lifted her, standing her on her feet.

She reached behind her back, her eyes darting to Lee and then Patrick, before settling on him. If she looked at him this would be okay. Her hands trembled as she unzipped her dress and let it slide to the floor at her feet.

CHAPTER 20: Patrick

Patrick couldn't take his eyes off Annie. She was more than beautiful. Her large breasts were encased in a black lace bra. The matching panties on her wide hips made his mouth water. "Let down your hair."

She reached above her, making the lush flesh of her chest rise, threatening to spill her tits from the tight bra. She undid her chignon, and her black tresses tumbled down around her shoulders.

"Beautiful." Lee took another sip of his drink, his eyes roving over her.

Patrick's possessiveness warred with his desire. He wanted to cover her up, but he also wanted her to strip bare so he could see all her beautiful golden skin. He glanced at Lee. Part of him liked watching this other man stare at Annie. He wanted this guy to see her, to see what belonged to him, but seeing was all he wanted the other man to do.

Lee stood and walked behind Annie. Patrick's fingers tightened around his glass. Annie's eyes locked with his, her knees shaking slightly as Lee's hands touched her shoulders.

"Relax, sugar." Lee stared at Patrick as he lowered his head and kissed her neck.

Patrick's lips curled, and he tossed back his drink to keep from shouting for the other man to get his fucking hands off her.

Lee grinned and Patrick almost launched himself across the room to introduce his fist to the cocky cowboy's face. This wasn't funny. Lee had done threesomes before this one. He had to know that this wasn't easy for Patrick. His hand tightened around the empty glass as he reminded himself that it wasn't Lee's fault. The other man had questioned him, and Patrick had insisted that he was fine with this. He was one dumb motherfucker.

"I think you're a little too far away from our friend." Lee's hands trailed down her arms, his long fingers skimming over the sides of her breasts as he moved her forward until she stood between Patrick's legs.

All thought fled as his gaze took in her body—the tan of her stomach and legs, and how it lightened to almost a cream color on her inner thighs. His finger trailed up and down the inside of her leg, marveling at her softness. Her skin was smooth as satin everywhere, but there, between her legs was the softest. It was as if no one had ever touched it but him.

"Hold on to me." Lee's voice was a rough whisper.

Patrick stared at the junction between her thighs, seeing the dampness soaking her panties. He inhaled the musky scent of her desire. He couldn't wait another minute to taste her. He leaned forward, trailing hot, open-mouthed kisses over her abdomen, and moving lower.

She moaned, her fingers tangling in his hair.

"Hold on to me." Lee took her hands.

Patrick looked up as the other man wrapped her arms around his neck. Lee's hands skimmed up and down her arms, but he didn't touch anywhere else. He nodded at Patrick.

Patrick appreciated the man's restraint. It wouldn't last, but he'd take it while he could.

CHAPTER 21: Annie

Annie shivered as Lee's rough hands skimmed up and down her arms, tickling along the sides of her breasts while Patrick's hot breath teased across her pussy. It felt great, but she needed more. "Please, Patrick. Touch me."

"Can't refuse a lady's request." Lee kissed her neck.

It was a quick, closed-mouth kiss, but before she had a chance to wonder why, Patrick's lips were on her. His mouth was hot and wet as he devoured her pussy through her underwear. The heat of his mouth and the scratch of the lace on her sensitive flesh made her tremble.

"You like that, don't you?" His lips pressed against her before he shifted away and slid his finger inside her panties, stroking along her seam.

"Oh...yes." She moaned, pushing against his hand.

"Hold her still." Patrick's voice was dark and commanding, making her body melt.

"Yes, sir." Lee wrapped one arm around her waist and tangled his other in her hair.

"Oh," she squeaked as Patrick yanked down her panties.

Without a word, Lee lifted her, and Patrick pulled her underwear off her feet and tossed them aside. Lee let her slide down his hard frame as he lowered her back to the floor, but Patrick grabbed her leg before her toes touched the carpet and tossed it over his shoulder.

"Patrick." She fell back against Lee, her hand tightening in Patrick's hair as Lee's arm pulled her flush against his body. She inhaled sharply as his long, hard cock pushed against the small of her back.

"Annie." Patrick looked up at her, as he kissed her thigh.

She stared into his gorgeous green eyes, and her words of surprise disappeared, replaced by lust.

"Did you want something?" He kissed along her leg, moving closer and closer to the juncture between her thighs.

"Please." She needed his mouth on her, his tongue inside her.

He grunted his reply as he spread her pussy lips and feasted, licking and teasing, stroking her folds before diving inside. His lips closed around her clit and sucked for one hot second before he lifted and flicked the tiny nub.

"Oh...oh." Her body writhed from pleasure as her leg tried to wrap around his neck and pull him closer.

"You gonna let her come so easily?" Lee's voice was like sandpaper against her ear. "Or you gonna make her earn it?"

"Please, Patrick." She hated waiting to orgasm, and he knew that.

He leaned away, wiping his face on his sleeve. "Lee's right." He dropped her leg from his shoulder.

"No. No. He's not." She almost cried.

"He is." Patrick slapped her pussy.

"Hey." She flushed because the sting felt pretty damn good.

"But he doesn't know you as well as I do." He stood, stepping closer until she was sandwiched between the two men. "Does he?"

"No." She barely said the word before his mouth was on hers.

He grabbed her chin, keeping her in place while his tongue invaded her, claiming her as his. His hand slid between her legs, and he slipped one finger inside her as his thumb caressed her clit. He whispered against her lips, "We can play a bit more before we have to stop. Can't we, babe?"

"Yes." She pulled free from Lee's hands and grabbed Patrick's head, pulling him back for another kiss.

"Take her," said Lee.

She stilled, her heart freezing in her chest because for one hot second she thought he meant for Patrick to fuck her. Then Lee stepped away, and Patrick pulled her close, his erection rubbing against her thigh. She leaned into him and kissed him, loving how his arms tightened around her. She lifted her hands to put them around his neck when Lee grabbed her arms, pulling them behind her back.

"Wait. What are you doing?" She felt something being wrapped around her wrists, and she yanked on her arms, falling against Patrick's chest.

His strong hands steadied her, holding her close.

"Handcuffs. Is that okay?" Lee loosened the restraint and waited for an answer.

"Annie?" Patrick stared at her.

"I...I don't know. This is all...."

"How about this." Lee undid her hands and then strode to the bed. He tossed the blanket on the floor before pulling some long straps of fabric from a table. He tied one end of the fabric to the headboard. "You can hold on like you're tied up."

"Do you want to do that?" Patrick studied her.

"Uhm...I wouldn't actually be tied up, right?" They'd done some bondage before, but everything was different with Lee here.

"No." Patrick smiled. "But you'll be punished if you let go. It'd probably be easier on you if I tie you up." His voice was rich and dark, reminding her of all those wonderful times with him.

"Okay." She trusted him completely.

"You sure?" he asked.

"You won't leave me, right?" She swallowed. She didn't think he would, but she'd never thought he'd want to share her with his friend either.

"Never." He grabbed her chin, his fingers tightening almost painfully. "I mean that, Annie. I'll do anything you want, except leave you."

"I'd never want you to leave."

"Good." Some of the tension slipped from his face. "Then are you okay with me tying you up?"

"Yeah. Whatever you think is best." She had to trust him on this and on everything tonight.

His mouth came down on hers, and his kiss was long and deep, marking her as his. She fell against him, giving herself to him fully. Nothing mattered but him. No one mattered but him and her. She was so lost to their passion that she barely noticed he'd lifted her as he strode across the room.

CHAPTER 22: Patrick

Patrick carried Annie to the huge bed, his tongue tangling with hers. She was his. His! And he was going to prove that to her as soon as he put her on the mattress.

"Wait." Lee walked toward them.

"For what?" Patrick would rather the guy stayed on the other side of the room.

"I want to take off her bra."

The muscle in Patrick's jaw did the cha-cha, but he let Annie slide down his body to the floor. Her soft moan of protest as he stepped aside made him feel a tiny bit better.

Lee moved behind her, lowering his face to her ear. "Is it okay if I undress you?"

She nodded, but her large brown eyes were unsure as she stared at Patrick.

"Thank you." Lee's hands rested on her waist. "But first...." They skimmed up her body, cupping her breasts and squeezing. "You have fabulous tits."

"Th...thank you." Annie's back was stiff. She was still scared.

Patrick couldn't be happier, and that made him feel like a heel.

"Hmm. Ethan was right. You are a stubborn one," muttered Lee.

"What do you mean by that?" She turned in his arms.

"I spoke with Ethan, and he said you were fiery and obstinate."

"Why did you talk to Ethan?" She glanced at Patrick.

He shrugged. He was as confused as she was.

"I wanted to know a little about you before we"—Lee grinned—"got to know each other really, really well." He winked at her.

Annie's cheeks heated at Lee's flirtation, and Patrick had to force himself not to step forward and punch the other man in the face. A broken and bloody nose would do a lot to minimize the guy's charm.

"I've met stubborn Annie." Lee's hands skimmed up and down her arms. "Now I want to meet fiery Annie."

"Oh...uhm...." She looked at Patrick again.

"Will you let her come out and play?" Lee's hands ran down her back to her ass. "I really want to see that side of you."

"I'm not an actor. I can't just change into a different character when you snap your fingers." Her eyes flashed with irritation.

"Apparently, you can." Patrick grinned. "Lee, meet fiery Annie."

"That wasn't quite what I had in mind." Lee frowned, but his blue eyes sparkled with laughter.

"Bitchy can be fiery too." Patrick shrugged.

"Patrick." She glared at him. "I was not being bitchy."

"Ah...I have to disagree." Lee winced jokingly when her eyes turned to him.

Patrick laughed and regretted it the moment the chuckle left his mouth because Annie's attention diverted to him, and he saw the challenge in her eyes. He'd forgotten that she also loved to prove him wrong.

"Sorry. I'll try harder for the fiery, passionate Annie." She gave him a superior look.

"Excellent." Lee rubbed his hands together. "We're going to have so much fun." He undid her bra with a quick touch of his fingers.

Annie gasped, and Patrick was a little afraid he had too. He wasn't a novice when it came to unfastening bras, but that'd been almost magical.

"Turn around and take it off." Lee's voice had grown gruffer.

She shifted so she faced the other man, her hands clasping the bra to her chest.

"Let it go, darlin'." Lee stared at her breasts.

Patrick had to fight to keep from snarling. Appreciating a woman's breasts was one thing, but Lee was almost drooling. His gaze shifted from the other man to Annie. Her eyes were wide and questioning. She was waiting for his permission. He wanted to step in front of her, to protect her, to block her from Lee's gaze, but instead he forced himself to nod.

She swallowed, but her chin jutted out as she let the bra slide down her arms and to the floor, setting her large, full breasts free for all to see.

"I'm going to give you a choice, darlin'." Lee's hand went to his pants, rubbing his cock. "You can wear those handcuffs I had earlier and suck Patrick's dick, or you can keep your hands unrestrained and suck mine."

Patrick held his breath, waiting for her to let the other man have it, but her jaw tightened as she looked at Patrick, blinking away the fire in her eyes. He wanted to remind her that she didn't have to do either of those things, but she should know that. She'd been the one who wanted this, not him.

"I'll give you a minute to decide." Lee walked to the other side of the room and grabbed a chair, carrying it and the handcuffs over to them. He put the chair down a few feet from the bed. "Time's up. Which is it?"

His heart stuttered almost to a stop, waiting for her answer. She'd wanted this. Would she pick Lee or him? He needed her answer, but he also wanted time to stop so he'd never have to hear her choose someone besides him.

"Patrick." She put her hands behind her back.

"Perfect." Lee walked over to her, clasping the cuffs around her wrists. "Do they feel okay?"

"Yeah." She kept her gaze on the wall across the room.

"Now on the bed you go." Lee lifted her, holding her naked body pressed to his and then lowering her onto her knees on the mattress.

Patrick couldn't stop himself from taking a step forward. He wanted to shove the other man away from her, but instead he took a huge, shaky breath. Soon, she was going to be a lot more than naked with this guy.

"Don't move." Lee smiled at Patrick as he took a step back. "Hmm. Almost perfect." He grabbed a few strands of Annie's hair, pulling it over her shoulders and letting it cascade over her breasts until just her nipples peeked from the dark tresses. "That's better."

Patrick had to agree it was. The whole scene was hot. Annie knelt naked and handcuffed on the bed. Her face right in front of his crotch, almost at eye level. The only problem he could see besides the other man in the room was that his dick was still in his pants.

"Stay right there." Lee strode across the room.

"You, okay?" he asked her.

"Yeah." She smiled up at him, but shadows lurked in her big brown eyes.

"You sure?"

"Ah...." Her eyes widened. "Patrick, did you know about this?"

He followed her gaze. "What the hell?"

Lee held Desiree's hand as he led her across the room. "You guys both know Des, right?"

"Yeah, but we agreed to a threesome, not a foursome." Patrick wanted fewer people in this room, not more.

"I know, but let's try this out." Lee winked at Patrick. "Trust me."

He turned to Annie. "Are you okay with this?"

"Ah...."

"Annie, darlin'," drawled Lee. "If you want another man touching you, you should be able to handle another woman touching your man. That's fair, right?"

"I don't want...." Her jaw clenched as she looked at Patrick. "Do you want this? I mean...this was your...you wanted...."

"I wanted what? What are you saying?" Hope fluttered in his heart. Did she not want to do this?

"Whatever Patrick wants." She stared at him, but he couldn't read her eyes.

"Whatever I want?" He almost shouted he wanted this to end before taking a deep breath. "If you're okay with it, then it's fine with me." He ground his teeth so tight that he swore they were going to disappear.

"Excellent." Lee sat on the chair, taking a sip of his drink. "Des, undress Patrick."

"What?" Annie's head snapped toward Lee.

"I undressed you, darlin'. It's only fair that Patrick gets to experience the same thing."

CHAPTER 23: Annie

Annie liked Desiree. They were friends—Club friends—but right now she wanted to slap the other woman. No, not slap her, beat her to a pulp, mar that perfect face of hers. Desiree was the most beautiful woman she'd ever seen, and she was touching Annie's man.

Desiree stood behind Patrick, her hands skimming up and down his strong back before making their way to his chest. Patrick's jaw was clenched, but his eyes were dark with passion, and there was no hiding the erection that pressed eagerly against his pants. Des's fingers teased along the buttons of his shirt, slowly undoing them one by one. Each time the other woman unfastened a button, her breasts rubbed against his back.

Annie's eyes dropped to his crotch, and he was getting bigger. She couldn't watch this for another second. "Are you going to undress him tonight?"

Patrick's eyebrows shot up.

"Gee," drawled Lee. "I think fiery Annie is making an appearance."

"I think so too." Desiree's voice was melodious and filled with humor.

"Whatever." Annie wanted to puke. "Just undo his pants." Once she had her lips around his cock, he wouldn't think about anyone but her.

"I see our little Annie is getting impatient." Lee stood and moved to the bed. "We have to let Desiree do her thing at her pace, but that doesn't mean the two of us can't find something to occupy ourselves." His fingers trailed up the outer side of her thigh.

"It's okay." She shifted away from him. "We can wait."

"I don't think so." Lee grabbed her by the waist. "I think we should remove the handcuffs." His gaze lifted to Patrick. "Is that okay with you? I'll tie her to the bed instead." He didn't wait for an answer.

Before Annie could even speak, Lee had removed the handcuffs and then she was pressed against his long, hard body for a second before she landed on her back on the bed. He grabbed her arm, tying the fabric which was hooked to the headboard around one wrist and then the other.

"Desiree, bring Patrick over here so they can see each other better," ordered Lee.

Annie's eyes narrowed as Des grabbed the now shirtless Patrick by the belt and pulled him to the foot of the bed. His face was hard and inscrutable. She had no idea if he was massively turned on or pissed off.

"There. Much better." Lee leaned over her, his hand skimming across her abdomen. "Should I touch her breasts?" He glanced at Patrick.

"Ask her." Patrick's jaw tightened even more.

"Do you want me to touch your breasts, Annie?"

"Ah...." Her gaze went to Patrick's.

"How about kiss them?" Lee's eyes darkened. "I'd really love to suck them. I'll even give them a little bite. Nothing too hard, but hard enough." He smiled. It was pure wicked temptation. "I can see you'd like that." He flicked her nipple.

Annie gasped, her gaze darting to Patrick who looked like a furious statue.

"I'm sure you enjoy it when Patrick does it." Lee rested his hand on her stomach. "But I bet I do it just a little different."

"I like how Patrick does it." She tried to focus on her boyfriend, but Lee's hand was hot and rough on her skin.

"I know you do, but you just might like how I do it too. It'll be good. I promise." His hand moved slowly upward. "A little different suction. A little different nip."

God, she was getting wet as his hand moved closer and closer to her breast. Her eyes darted to Patrick again. He didn't look like he was enjoying this, but this had been his idea.

Lee glanced at him, a slight frown on his handsome lips.

"You should taste her," said Desiree.

"You're right." Lee's blue eyes sparkled as he lowered his face to Annie's stomach.

She inhaled sharply as Lee kissed across her abdomen, making his way toward her breasts. God, it felt good but wrong.

"Do you like watching this, Patrick?" asked Lee before running his tongue along the underside of her breast.

"She's the voyeur, not me." Patrick's tone was dark and rough.

"That's right." Lee sat up. "He likes to do and you"—he grinned at her—"like to watch." His eyes locked with Annie's. "Des, give this voyeur something to watch."

"Yes, sir." Desiree winked at her.

Annie almost snarled as the other woman's fingers trailed over Patrick's dick through his pants. His nostrils flared, but he didn't move.

"You like watching but I bet you like being busy while you watch. How about if I eat your pussy"—Lee pulled her leg away from her other one, opening her for everyone to see—"while you watch Des suck Patrick's dick?"

"No." She had no idea how it escaped, but that word just wouldn't stay inside any longer.

"No?" Lee leaned back, a smirk on his face. "No to what?"

"You're an ass." Her gaze snapped to his. "No to this. All of it." She tugged on her restraints. "Unhook me. I'm done."

"Done with what?" Lee gave her a confused look, but his eyes sparkled with amusement. "Des touching your man?"

"Yes, but not just that." She yanked on the restraints. "Untie me. I'm done with this. I don't want you."

"Okay." Lee stood. "I can grab another guy from the Club to take my place in your threesome."

"No," she almost screamed. She was so ready to cry. She'd storm away except no one would untie her. "I don't want another man. I don't want a threesome." Her mouth dropped open, and her eyes shot to Patrick. "Oh, God. I'm sorry." She blinked, but she couldn't keep the tears inside any longer. It was over. He wouldn't want her anymore. She couldn't keep up with his kink.

"Praise the Lord. Finally, the truth." Lee walked to the chair and sat, tossing back his drink before patting his leg. Desiree walked across the room and sat on his lap. "You are the two most stubborn people I have ever met, and I live in Texas where bullheadedness is in our genes."

"They sure are." Desiree laughed. "I'm going to get a drink. Anyone want one?"

"I do." Lee handed her his glass.

"Annie." Patrick moved over to her, ignoring the other couple. "You...you don't want a threesome?"

"No." She shook her head. "I'm sorry. I should've told you, but...but you wanted to do this, and I didn't want to disappoint you." Now that she'd started, the words tumbled from her. "I thought I'd be okay with it...be able to go through with it as long as you were here, but...."

"I wanted one?" He poked his chest with his finger. "Why would you think I wanted one? I hate threesomes."

"You hate...." She was so confused. "Then why did you suggest it?"

"I thought you wanted it." He shrugged.

"You were right, Lee." Desiree sat back down on his lap, sipping a drink. "But I won on the time."

"Only by a couple of minutes." Lee grinned. "I thought Fiery Annie would've shown up sooner." He laughed. "Hell, she's so stubborn I thought I was going to have to lick that sweet pussy to get one of you two assholes to call a stop to the game." His eyes twinkled as they met Patrick's. "I was hoping she'd stop me because I didn't want to eat your fist."

"If you had done any more, you would've." Patrick looked a little sheepish. "Sorry, I got you involved in this, but thanks."

"No problem, but you were lucky you approached me. I don't think some of the others would've been game to stop." Lee's gaze drifted to Annie.

"Could one of you please untie me." She was the only one naked in the room, and it was a little embarrassing.

"Right." Patrick moved to the headboard.

"Wait." Lee's hand caressed Desiree's leg. "It'd be a shame to waste this room."

"I don't want a foursome either." She tipped her head at her arms. "Patrick, the restraints."

"Hold on." He held up his hand, his eyes still on Lee. "Let's hear what he has to say."

"You like to watch, and we don't mind putting on a show." Lee kissed Desiree's neck as his hand cupped her breast. "Do we, darlin'?"

CHAPTER 24: Annie

Annie's heart pounded in her chest as Lee's hand squeezed Desiree's breast. His blue eyes locked with Annie's as his other hand skimmed up and under Des's skirt.

"Annie?" Patrick's eyes were dark with passion. "Do you want to leave?"

She stared up at him, her throat dry. "Do you?" It came out almost like a croak.

"Don't." He ran his hand over her cheek. "Don't fucking do this again." He grabbed the back of her neck. "I almost let someone else touch you because I thought that's what you wanted." He tangled his hand in her hair and jerked back her head. "Tell me what *you* want, not what you think I want to hear."

"I want to watch." All she'd ever really wanted was to watch with him.

"Excellent." A slow sexy smile spread across his face as he kicked off his shoes and sat on the bed.

"Aren't you going to remove your pants?" She wanted him as naked as she was so they could play while they watched.

"Not yet." He ducked under her arm and crawled behind her spreading his legs and pulling her back against his chest. "Now. Watch the show."

It was his favorite thing to say to her when they were at the Club. He'd started it the first time they'd met, and those three simple words made wetness gush from her. Sometimes, the damn man would say them innocently when they were watching TV. Then he'd look at her, smirking as she wiggled on the couch like a perverse version of Pavlov's dog.

His large, warm hands started on her waist, caressing, and teasing along her skin. She leaned more heavily against him, straightening her spine so her boobs pressed forward, hinting at what she wanted.

"I think she wants some breast play," said Lee. "Sound good to you, Des?"

"Definitely." Desiree grinned at Annie as she got off Lee's lap.

Lee unzipped her dress slowly, kissing his way down her back. Desiree's eyes locked with Annie's as Lee helped the cloth over her hips, letting it fall to the floor. Annie's gaze wandered down the other woman's perfect body. Desiree had long legs that led to rounded hips and a tiny waist. Her breasts were large and firm with pert nipples that'd already tightened into hard little buds.

"Do you like her breasts?" Patrick's hands teased beneath Annie's boobs. "See how her nipples are hard." His voice was a rough whisper in her ear. "Do you know what that does to a man? What it tells him?" His fingers skimmed over her nipples that were so hard even that teasing touch made her gasp.

"No." She shook her head. She did know. She wasn't a fool, but she also knew their game. She wanted him, needed him to show her.

"I think you do." He smiled against her cheek.

"I don't. You need to tell me."

"Do I?"

"Yes." It was barely a sound as she watched Lee's hands wander over Desiree's body.

"No." His fingers circled her nipple, but she needed more pressure. "Lee, tell Annie what hard nipples do to a man."

"My pleasure." Lee stood, grinning at them as his gaze roved over Annie.

His blue eyes were hot and dark, and she shifted against Patrick, wanting him to touch her, to kiss her while she watched Lee with Desiree.

"Well, darlin'." Lee's hands slid up Des's waist, cupping her breasts. "These hard little nipples"—he rolled them between his fingers and thumbs—"tell me that this woman is ready." One of his hands skimmed down her belly. "For me to fuck her." He cupped her pussy, pulling her against him and lifting her off the floor as his other hand pinched her nipple. Desiree's head dropped back on his shoulder, and she moaned, her legs falling open for his touch.

"Are you ready, Annie?" Patrick's hand skimmed over her mound but stopped, his fingers just inches away from her pussy.

"You tell me." She spread her legs, giving him better access.

"Is she ready for you, Patrick?" Lee's hand worked between Desiree's legs, sliding between her slick folds, and teasing her clit. Her red lips parted, and her cheeks flushed as her hand clenched Lee's wrist, holding him to her as her hips undulated with his rhythm.

Patrick slid one long finger between her folds, and Annie moaned, her eyes drifting partially closed.

"She is, but I think she should wait a bit." He rubbed her clit. "I don't think she fully understands what women do to men."

"I do." She rocked against his hand. "I don't need to wait. I understand." She needed to come is what she needed.

"I don't think I can believe you." Patrick's hands move to her breast tweaking her nipple. "You lied when you said you wanted a threesome."

"That's not fair." She shifted, turning in his arms to glare at him. "So did you."

He kissed her, hard and demanding as his tongue thrust into her mouth, claiming her as his.

She wiggled, pulling at the restraints. She needed to hold him, touch him. "Untie me," she whispered against his lips.

"Not yet." He grabbed her head and turned her back toward Lee and Desiree. "The show's just starting."

"I've seen enough." She was hot and ready for his touch.

"Oh, come on, now, Annie. We've barely started," said Lee. "Maybe you should give her a little one, Patrick."

"No. She can wait to come."

"I like his idea better," she muttered under her breath.

"I'm sure you do," Patrick chuckled. "But unfortunately for you, you're mine and not Lee's." He skimmed his hands up and down her inner thighs. "Why don't you let Des come? I'm sure Annie would like to see that."

"Sounds good to me." Desiree grinned as her hips continued to move against Lee's hand.

"After you suck my dick." Lee grabbed her chin, pulling her face toward his and kissing her. "I've been on edge for ages waiting on these two dumbasses to admit they didn't want a threesome."

"Poor baby." Des reached behind her, stroking his cock.

"That's it, darlin'." Lee let go of her, and she turned, running her hand along all his smooth skin.

Annie's heart pounded as the other woman kissed her way down Lee's gorgeous chest, before kneeling before him. She ran her long red nails across the bulge in his pants.

"You like this don't you?" Patrick's voice was rough in her ear.

"Yes." She couldn't tear her eyes away, as Des unzipped Lee's pants, freeing his long, hard cock.

Desiree licked up and down the shaft before taking the tip in her mouth. Lee's eyes were like blue glass, as he stared at Desiree. His hand cupped the back of her head, pushing her onto his cock. Her mouth widened, taking him deep into her throat until his dick disappeared.

"Jesus," she whispered. Des was so tiny, and that cock wasn't little, but somehow it fit all the way in.

"Fuck." Lee made a guttural sound and then his hips began to thrust as his hands tangled for a moment in Desiree's hair before he dropped his arms to his sides. She pulled away from his dick, gasping a moment and then went right back, swallowing his cock.

Lee grunted. The sound so primal that Annie's pussy throbbed. Patrick's breath came in pants now, his hands skimming along her legs. His hard cock pressed against Annie's back. He was as mesmerized as she was with the show. She wiggled, rocking her ass against his dick.

"Watch...the...show." He groaned in her ear, but his hips thrust against her.

"Untie my hands."

He didn't move.

She turned, staring at him. "I want to suck your dick while you watch."

His eyes dropped to hers, and she almost combusted from the heat. He leaned to the side, unfastening one restraint and then the other. She was free. She shifted, so she was on her knees facing him. His dick pressed against his pants, large and more than ready to come out and play.

"Oh, that must hurt." She ran her finger along his hard cock.

"You have no idea." His words were rough and desperate.

"Let me help." She glanced up at him as she unbuttoned and unzipped his pants. The grunts and sucking sounds that filled the room made her wetter. She bent, running her tongue along the top of his dick.

"Annie." He grabbed her hair, forcing her eyes to his.

"What do you want, Patrick?" She blew across his cock.

"Suck my dick." His hand tightened in her hair.

She knew him well enough to know that he loved to play, but when the tip of his dick was this red, he was done playing.

Too bad for him because she wasn't. It was time to give him a taste of his own game. "Okay, but you need to watch the show, or I stop."

CHAPTER 25: Patrick

"Don't you dare stop." Patrick would either die of frustration or cry like a baby if Annie didn't suck his dick. He'd been furious and turned on all night as he'd tried to keep his temper in check every time Lee had touched her. Now that he knew Annie didn't want a threesome, everything disappeared except his lust. He was so relieved that he wasn't about to lose the best thing that'd ever happened to him that he ached for her. She only wanted him, and he needed her lips on his dick. Now.

"Then you'd better watch the show."

"I'd rather watch you." He loved seeing her suck him off. Her dark eyes always sparkled with mischief and desire as she gave him the most exquisite pleasure.

"Then I stop." She puckered her lips and gave his dick a playful kiss before starting to sit up.

"No." He almost shouted as he grabbed her head and pushed her back toward his crotch. "I'll watch the show." Fuck, he'd never realized what a shit thing that was to say.

He forced his eyes away from her face and his entire body stiffened. Lee's cock slid in and out of Desiree's mouth as she bobbed and sucked, her fingers caressing his balls. The other man's hands tangled in her hair, holding her in place while he fucked her face. Patrick gritted his teeth to keep from coming all over Annie's face as her hand wrapped around his cock, and she slid him inside her mouth. He groaned, adding to the sounds of sex and pleasure that already filled the room, as that hot wet haven surrounded his dick. She started sucking, softly at first, but the pressure increased as she slid him deeper. His hips thrust toward her, and she gagged slightly before sucking him harder.

His eyes dropped partway closed, and he tangled his fingers in her hair, trying not to force the pace but failing miserably. Lee's eyes were closed and his head back. The man was close to coming. Patrick bit down on his lip to try and push back his orgasm as Annie sucked him deeper, his cock sliding into her tight throat.

Desiree slowly moved down Lee's dick until her nose was almost against his pubes.

He gasped as Annie focused on his tip, sucking hard. She skimmed a fingernail along his balls, scratching gently.

Lee shouted, his hips bucking. Desiree slid off him, and his cum splattered against her face.

"Fuck me." He couldn't take much more.

Desiree smiled at him as she took Lee's cock in her hand and licked him clean.

That was it. It was too much. He grabbed Annie's face with both hands, holding her still as he thrust into her mouth. His body stiffened as he came. Instead of sliding off him, Annie licked and swallowed. He grunted as the pressure of her throat made him spurt again.

"Fuck." He'd never come so hard. He flopped back against the headboard as she pulled off his cock, her brown eyes sparkling. "I love you." He'd never felt like this for anyone.

"You'd better." She leaned down and licked his cock, cleaning up his cum.

"Annie." His dick twitched at the hot roughness of her tongue.

"Nice, very nice." Lee's deep voice made them both jump.

For a moment, Patrick had forgotten everything but her.

"Rest up but make it quick." Lee swatted Annie's ass.

"Hey." She turned toward him.

Lee handed them each a drink. "We're about to start round two."

CHAPTER 26: Annie

"It's going to be a quickie." Annie grinned at Patrick. He may be satiated, but she was tight and on edge.

"Oh no. No quickies tonight." Lee strode to Des who was sitting on the chair. They were both completely naked. His semi-flaccid penis bounced between his legs as he offered his hand to Desiree. "It's your turn, my dear."

"Lovely." Des finished her drink and put her hand in his. "Lead the way."

"Patrick, get the button," said Lee. "It's to your right."

"Got it." Patrick drank half his whiskey and put it on the nightstand before leaning over and pressing a button on the wall.

"What is he doing?" She couldn't stop herself from running her hand up his back. All that hot male flesh almost demanded that she touch it.

"You'll see." A motor hummed, and Patrick glanced at Lee. "Tell me when?"

Annie turned, watching a bar lower from the ceiling. She'd seen them before but always from up above in the viewing areas. It looked different from down here—more ominous—and her body throbbed. Desiree was about to be strung up—helpless to whatever Lee wanted to do to her—and Annie was going to have a front row seat. Her hand drifted between her legs, slowly teasing her clit.

"That's good." Lee tossed back his drink before bending to put his glass on the floor and giving Annie a very nice view of his ass.

Her fingers rubbed a little faster. Des watched him too, a hungry expression in her gaze. Neither of the women had come, and Lee was a fine-looking man, especially without his clothes.

He straightened, grinning at the look on Desiree's face. "Don't worry, darlin'. You'll get all of me but not just yet."

"Tease." Des pouted, but her eyes sparkled with humor.

"You know it." Lee wiggled his fingers in a come-hither motion. "Hands."

Des extended her arms, and he wrapped a restraint around her wrists.

"Good?" he asked.

"A little looser, please."

"You got it." His long fingers caressed her wrists as they loosened the restraints. "How's that?"

"Perfect." Desiree almost purred. Her voice was seductive like warm honey drizzled over a naked body.

He stepped closer as he raised her arms above her head. He lifted her off her toes, and her body fell against his before he hooked her to the bar that was suspended from the ceiling. He let her slide down his frame until she was on her toes. "Now for some toys."

Annie's fingers moved faster as Des's eyes met hers. The other woman's face was flushed, and her chest rose and fell with her breath.

"Do you want something, Patrick?" Lee stood by a cabinet.

"A vibrator."

Annie jumped as his deep voice rumbled in her ear.

"I already have the restraints." He grabbed her hand, pulling it from between her legs.

"Patrick," she moaned. "Please." She tugged on her wrist. She'd been so close.

"Not yet. That pussy is mine to play with."

"Then you'd better get busy." She was done waiting. She needed release now.

"Oh, she's so lucky you aren't her Dom." Lee slapped Desiree's ass.

"Annie could never last a day with a Dom." Patrick laughed. "She's way too bossy."

"Hey." She knew she was bossy, but it hurt knowing he thought that about her too. "Don't say—" Her protest turned into a squeak as he lifted her, dropping her on her stomach with her head at the foot of the bed. "What are you...?"

He grabbed her leg, tying it to the bedpost with the restraints that had been on her hand.

"You're tying my legs?" Oh, this was getting interesting.

"Yep." He hooked the other one.

Lee stopped at the foot of the bed, his cock right at her face and tossed a box onto the mattress. "Vibrator."

"Get her hands for me." Patrick took the toy from the box, unwrapping it. Everything at the Club was new unless they brought their own.

"Gladly." Lee stared at her.

She looked up at him, getting an eyeful of his dick.

"It's a damn shame we aren't sharing. She's got a great mouth–wide and lush." Lee's cock began to harden.

"Well, we aren't." Patrick's tone was firm, and the possessiveness made her heart light. "Just tie her hands."

"To the bedposts?" Lee grabbed her wrists.

"No," said Patrick. "Tie them together and to the top, but don't string her up."

"Patrick." She looked over her shoulder at him. "What are you...?"

"On your elbows." Lee dropped her hands and bent, grabbing another restraint from under the bed and wrapping it around her hands. "How's that feel?" He looked down at her.

"Okay. I guess. What are you—"

"You'll see." Patrick swatted her ass.

"Hey." Her tone was more turned-on than angry. She loved it when he got a little rough.

"Okay works for me." Lee shifted forward as he raised her arms, putting his dick literally right in her face.

Patrick straddled her, his large body surrounding hers. As he leaned down, his hot breath teased her ear. "Do you want to suck him? Taste him?" His fingers played between her legs.

"No." She didn't. "Only you."

"Good answer." He slid one finger inside her and swatted her ass again, sending a jolt of pleasure to her pussy.

"Oh, God. Patrick," she moaned.

"Soon, baby." His finger pumped inside her, and she pressed into the bed, searching for some release.

Lee hooked her hands to the tether at the top of the bed, making it taut but not tight. "That good?"

Patrick got off the bed and looked her over. "Perfect." He moved behind her again, and she tensed as the sound of the vibrator filled the air.

Des's eyes sparkled as she watched them.

"Let's begin." Lee grabbed a small flogger from the floor next to the bed and walked around Desiree, dancing it across her breasts, over her abdomen, and then snapping it against her ass.

CHAPTER 27: Patrick

Patrick's dick was already swelling again. He'd never seen Annie hotter than right now. She was tied to the bed, her legs spread wide with moisture glistening on her inner thighs and her lush ass just waiting for his hand. Damn, she needed a spanking more than any woman he'd ever met. She'd made him question everything—her feelings for him and how he was going to feel about them after the threesome that she'd never freaking wanted. Annie never kept her opinion to herself. He had to find out why she had this time.

The slap of the flogger and a sharp gasp from Desiree made him turn. Lee stood behind her, the flogger dancing over her naked butt and thighs with every twist of his wrist. Her gasps turned into moans as Lee got on his knees, grabbing her thighs, and burying his face between her legs.

Patrick's hand skimmed down Annie's back, and she jumped. "I should be crushed. You forgot about me."

"I...I didn't." Her eyes were locked on the scene before her.

Des's face was a mask of ecstasy, and her soft mewls and moans made Patrick's dick harden even more.

"You did, but you won't again." He ran the vibrator up her inner thigh as his other hand squeezed her ass. "I think you need to be spanked."

"Why?" She wiggled her butt, showing him that she was more than eager for the spanking.

He licked his finger, running it along her butthole as he leaned over her. "We almost had a threesome," he said against her ear.

"I...I thought you wanted it."

"I want you to be happy." His hand slipped between her legs.

"I am happy." She pulled her eyes away from the scene and stared at him over her shoulder. "With you. Just you and me."

"I'm glad." He kissed her neck while his fingers teased her clit until she moaned. "I'm very glad, but you need to be honest about what you want and don't want." He slid his finger back to her ass and pushed it inside her butthole just a little. "Understand?"

"Yes," she gasped.

Des screamed in release, and Annie's gaze went to the other couple. Lee still had his face buried between Desiree's legs.

"We're falling behind." He sat up, slapping her butt as he pressed the vibrator along her pussy. "Time to get this nice and wet."

CHAPTER 28: Annie

Annie's entire body stiffened as Patrick slid the vibrator inside of her. The sensations teased her sensitive flesh, making her tremble. His finger probed her butthole, slipping inside just a little as the vibrator stroked along her pussy.

Lee stood, wiping his face on his arm before grabbing Des's hips. "You ready for my cock, baby?"

"Yes." Desiree's eyes were half closed from her orgasm.

Annie shivered as Patrick teased her with the vibrator, stroking inside her and then pulling it out and pressing it against her clit. She needed more. She needed to feel him. She wiggled her ass, causing his finger to dip in a little farther, and she clenched around him.

"Fuck, Annie." His voice was guttural with desire.

"Nooo." She moaned as he pulled his finger out of her. "Please, no." She needed him.

"Yes." He grabbed her hair, sliding his cock between her butt cheeks. "I'm going to fuck your ass now"—he grabbed a condom from the bed—"and then I'm going to fuck your pussy."

"Yes." God, yes. Hallelujah and yippee.

"Watch the show." He slid his dick along her seam.

She almost gushed when he put his hand between her legs, his calloused fingers dipping into her sensitive flesh and capturing her wetness before smearing it around her asshole. He moved his hand, replacing it with his hot, hard cock.

She moaned, dropping her forehead to the bed.

"Watch the show." He grabbed her hair, pulling back her head.

Lee's large hands held Desiree's hips as he fucked her. Her breasts swayed from his thrusts and then Patrick was pushing his dick into her ass.

She whimpered. They'd done this before, and she loved it, but he was so big.

His hand caressed her back. "Relax, baby." He pumped into her, slow and gentle, going a little farther with each thrust. His hand drifted between her legs, teasing her clit.

She rolled with his tempo, losing herself to the back and forth and the teasing of her clit. Her gaze locked on Lee as he fucked Desiree hard and fast.

"Fuck." Patrick slid almost all the way inside her and then pulled out, his rhythm still slow and gentle, but his thrusts were longer and deeper. He shifted a little, grabbing the vibrator from the bed.

"Patrick...." The word was both a plea and a warning. She knew what was coming, and she wanted it, needed it, but it'd be such exquisite torture.

"Annie...." His tone was amused. "Take it like a good girl." He slid the vibrator along her pussy.

"Ohh." Her body rubbed against it, making her ass rock with his movements.

"That's it, baby." He pushed the vibrator inside her.

"Oh...Patrick." She shook as the sensations rocked through her from everywhere. The pain from his hand wrapped in her hair warred with the pleasure of his dick filling her ass and the toy humming between her legs.

"Fuck, Annie. You feel so good." He groaned as he revved up the vibrator to full speed.

"Oh...god...Patrick." Her body shook, clasping onto him. It was too much. "Stop, please."

"Safeword," he grunted as he grabbed her hips, leaving the vibrator pulsing inside her as he fucked her harder. "God, this feels fucking amazing."

His cock and the vibrator filled her, as his thrusts rocked the bed. Pleasure shot through her body in waves. She couldn't hold back any longer. "Patrick," she screamed as she came, bucking under him as her entire body clenched down on the vibrator and his cock.

He groaned, stopping his thrusts. His arms shook as his fingers dug into her hips, holding her tight until her body relaxed. Then he pulled out of her ass.

"Oh," she moaned, the sound becoming a whimper as he removed the vibrator.

He swatted her butt. "Time for round two."

CHAPTER 29: Patrick

Desiree screamed again as Lee rocked faster and harder into her. Patrick didn't even care. All he wanted was to get inside Annie's pussy. His entire world focused on that sweet bit of flesh between her legs. He reached behind him, untying her ankles from the restraints and bending her legs under her so she was kneeling with her top half pressed against the mattress. Her body was languid like putty from her orgasm, but he'd have her tense again in a minute.

He spread her ass and buried his face in her pussy. She was more than wet. At the first taste of her, he licked faster, her desire a delicious blend of sweet and spice, just like her.

"Oh...oh...." She wiggled a little but not enough.

He teased her clit with his tongue and then shifted her higher so he could latch on to her little nub and suck.

"Fuck...Patrick." She squirmed, trying to get away from him.

His fingers tightened on her, and he sucked harder because he was never letting her go. He'd do whatever he had to do in order to imprint this night into her brain.

"Patrick. I need...."

He leaned up. Her fingers shook, unable to get a grasp on the sheets, and her back was stiff. He had her on the edge of pleasure and pain.

Lee and Desiree sat in the chair, which was now in front of the bed, watching.

He grabbed her hair, forcing her to look at the other couple. "You're the show now, Annie." He turned her head and kissed her, plunging into her mouth and letting her feel his need, his dominance. "You're mine. Only mine." He pulled the condom off, tossed it on the floor, and positioned himself at her opening. He slid into her in one hard thrust.

"Oh...." Her body tightened, and she trembled beneath him.

He gritted his teeth to keep from coming as her body squeezed his. He'd known she was getting close again, but he hadn't realized she was that close.

"Please." She shifted, trying to get him to move, to make her come.

"Not yet." He let go of her hair and pressed down on her back, holding her still.

"Patrick," she whined.

"Not yet," he repeated through clenched teeth.

She groaned but didn't move again. When her breathing was back to normal, he began to move in slow, shallow thrusts that sparked their passion again.

"Oh...yes." She rocked against him, and his movements became longer and harder, taking them both back to the edge.

He patted the bed, finding the vibrator. He turned it on and slid it between her legs, teasing her clit.

"Patrick...." Her body bucked at the touch. "God...stop.... It's too much." Sweat ran down her back as she moaned and thrust against him, her body tightening around his cock.

"Safeword, Annie." He grunted as he pumped into her. She was so wet and hot and slick, and she felt fucking perfect.

"No." She buried her face in the bed, taking everything he gave to her.

She never backed down or used the safeword that'd stop or slow their pleasure. She took everything head on in life. She was amazing, and she was his. She belonged to him. He loved her, completely and forever. He pulled the vibrator away from her pussy and she cried out. "This is the closest you're ever going to get to being fucked by two men because"—he wrapped his hand in her hair and pulled back her head as he lowered his lips to her ear—"you're mine. Do you hear me?"

"Y-yes," she whispered.

"You belong to me." He let go of her hair. "That means this pussy and this ass are mine." He wanted to pound his chest like a caveman but instead he slid the vibrator into her butthole.

CHAPTER 30: Annie

Annie's eyes locked with Lee's as the vibrator slid into her ass. She'd never felt this full and this on edge. "Please...." She was nothing but a bundle of raw nerves. She couldn't come again. She might die, combusting with pleasure, but she wouldn't say her safeword. She didn't want this to stop. She enjoyed ass play, but this was more than fun. This was exquisite. Patrick's hard thrusts filled her pussy as the vibrator slid in and out, almost gently in comparison, sending those lovely vibrations pulsing through her core.

His hands came down on either side of her. His body trapped the vibrator deep inside her ass as he continued to thrust into her. "You want two men, Annie?" His lips pressed against her ear, his words hard and on edge. "I can be two men. I can be rough." He fucked her harder, sliding her across the bed. "And gentle." His pace slowed as he rocked into her, kissing her neck and ear. "I can be whatever you need."

"Yes." She turned, her mouth catching his, their tongues tangling. She pulled back just a little, her lips still pressed against his. "Only you, Patrick."

His green eyes locked with hers for a moment as if searching for the truth. She didn't even blink because it was the truth. He was all she wanted, and all she had ever wanted. Someone she could rely on. Someone she could trust to stay by her side.

The green of his eyes turned almost black with need. He straightened, his thrusts getting faster and harder, pushing deeper inside of her. His fingers dug into her hips and his other hand swatted her ass. "Honesty." He spanked her again. "Always."

The force of his slaps caused the vibrator to shift. It now pressed against the thin layer of skin that separated the two passages, causing his cock to rub along the small toy.

"Fuck." He groaned as he grabbed her hips with both hands. His pace became frenzied as he raced toward his climax.

Her fingernails dug into her palms as her body clasped around him, trying to keep him inside of her. She almost whimpered as he slipped away but then he was back, long, and hard. She screamed as her body exploded. Her pussy squeezing his dick, never wanting this to end. He grunted as he thrust into her again and again before he stiffened. His hips pumped a few more times as he emptied himself inside of her.

He pulled the vibrator from her ass and tossed it on the floor before leaning over her and untying her wrists. He collapsed on the bed, pulling her into his arms.

"I missed this." She snuggled against him.

"Missed what?" He kissed the top of her head. "We have sex all the time, but I'm definitely okay with doing it more." He grinned against her hair.

"Not the sex."

"Damn." He pulled her closer. "Then what do you miss, Annie? The truth." His voice had grown serious.

She rested her cheek against his chest, feeling shy for the first time in forever. "This closeness. I feel like you've been pulling away from me after sex."

"I have not been pulling away from you." He tipped his head, looking at her.

"You have too. You want honesty? I'm giving it to you." She touched his lips. "I love you, but you've been distant after sex. I thought...I thought you were losing interest in me." She couldn't stop the tears from welling up in her eyes.

"Never." He kissed her fingers.

"Then why have you been distant?" She needed to know. She couldn't live with the doubts.

"I...." He sighed. "I thought you wanted more."

"More? More what?" She had no idea what he was talking about.

"More this." He waved his hand as if showing off the room. "More kink."

"Why would you think...?" She sat up and then stilled, her eyes landing on Lee and Desiree who sat on the chair watching them.

"Don't stop on our account." Lee smirked. "This isn't just porn. We care about the characters."

Des laughed and Lee winked at her, his hand running over her ass.

"You're fucking hilarious." Patrick pulled Annie back into his arms.

"I think our time here is done." Lee lifted Desiree, swatting her backside as she bent to gather her clothes.

Lee pulled on his pants and grabbed Des's hand as they walked across the room, stopping in the doorway. "Next time—"

"There won't be a next time," said Patrick.

"Don't be hasty. Think about it a bit." Lee's eyes raked over Annie. "We could do same rules, except I think I should get to give the two of you orders."

"You mean, you'd tell us what to do?" Annie glanced at Patrick.

"Yep. I tell you what position and when to suck, spread them, lick, and all sorts of fun things." Lee's grin deepened.

"And we have to obey?" Annie's eyes sparkled.

"Lord, help me." Patrick groaned.

"No." She shook her head. It sounded intriguing to her, but he wasn't interested. "There won't be a next time."

"Do you want to do that?" Patrick grabbed her chin.

"Do you?"

"I asked first." His green eyes searched hers. "And this time, tell me what you want. How you feel. Not what you think I want to hear."

She hesitated. He'd just admitted that he thought she wanted more kink. She loved these games and scenes but not nearly as much as she loved him.

"Annie, we need to be open and honest about everything we want to try. Then we can decide as a couple what we will and won't do."

She nodded. "I think it sounds like fun, but if you don't, that's fine too."

"I do."

"You sure? You didn't seem like you were interested."

"That's because I know Lee and he can be a twisted, commanding motherfucker." He shot the other guy a disgusted look.

"That's true." Lee's chest puffed up a bit with pride.

"And he'll have to remember that I'm not a sub." Patrick gave the other man a look that made it clear that was not something he'd allow.

"Yeah, that'll be hard, but I'm sure you'll be quite eager to do everything I suggest. I promise it'll be hot, and I also promise to beat your score."

"Our score?" She glanced from one to the other as Patrick groaned.

"Our orgasm score." Patrick's eyes gleamed. "Lee's going to make you—"

"No. You'll make her. I'll watch." Lee's hand ran over Desiree's hip. "With help from Des of course to take the edge off. But yes, I kept score." He smirked. "I tend to do that a lot. So next time, Patrick will have to make you come more than three times, and you'll have to make him come more than twice."

"Oh. That does sound...interesting." Her heart raced, and her blood began to heat. She ran her leg up his and then placed it across his thighs.

"Seems she's ready to go again after just talking about it." Lee's grin widened. "I can't wait to come back into town."

"We never agreed." She leaned up on her arms, staring at Patrick. "Are you sure?"

"Yes. I love you, and as long as no other man touches you, I want to do and try whatever you want."

She studied him for a long minute, and all she saw in his eyes was love. "Lee, we're in."

"Excellent." Lee rubbed his hands together. "I can't wait."

"You'll have to." She glanced at the cowboy. "Close the door behind you."

"I love fiery Annie." Lee laughed.

"Don't love her too much; she's mine." Patrick pulled her closer and rolled on top of her.

CHAPTER 31: Annie

The door closed, and Annie stared at Patrick. They still had things to talk about. "It really hurt me when you were distant. I thought...I thought you wanted to end it." Her voice cracked.

"Never." He wiped a tear off her cheek.

"You don't need alone time?" She knew she was bossy and could be a bit much sometimes. Her brothers had told her that all her life, and then they'd all left her.

"Sometimes."

"Oh." It was like he'd stabbed her in the heart.

"Don't be like that." He kissed her softly. "I love you. I love being with you, but we're different people. We both need some alone time, and you know it."

She nodded, smiling just a little because he was right, but she still felt like crying. "I know. I just don't like hearing you say it."

"Too bad because from now on I'm going to be more honest too. I swear. If I don't want to do something, I'll tell you."

"You'd better." She slapped his chest playfully.

"I'll start with those painting classes." He grimaced.

"I thought you liked those." She really enjoyed those classes.

"Hardly."

"You get to drink wine."

"I drink whisky, not wine."

"Okay." She frowned. "You don't have to go anymore."

"You're not mad?" His eyes searched hers.

"No." She was a little disappointed, but she didn't want him doing things he didn't like. Plus, she wasn't one to dwell on the negative when it could be a positive. "And it'll give me time to hang out with Chelsea a little more."

"Hmm. In that case, maybe I should go with you."

"Stop it." She slapped him again. "She's one of my best friends."

"She's a flirt."

"Yes, but flirting is healthy, and wondering what we're up to will make you all hot and horny by the time I get home."

"I'm always hot and horny for you." He tipped his head and ran his tongue across her nipple.

"I know, and I love that." She reached between them, squeezing his growing erection.

"Woman, spread those legs. Now." The guttural tone of his voice made her body gush.

"Yes, sir." She wrapped one leg over his hip.

He slid inside her slowly, letting her feel every hard inch of him, but then he stopped. He brushed the hair away from her face. "I love you, Annie Argotos."

Her heart wanted to melt from the look of adoration in his eyes and burst from happiness. She'd thought she'd lost him, lost this. "I love you too, Patrick Westman."

He kissed her, shifting his hips and making love to her slowly, worshiping every part of her with his touch.

"Please, Patrick." She rocked against him. She enjoyed a nice slow fuck...for a bit. Then she was ready to pick up the pace so she could come.

"Shhh." He kissed her again, keeping his movements slow and steady.

"Oh," she moaned as he shifted, his cock rubbing against her G-spot.

"Found it." His eyes sparkled as he pumped into her, over and over, each time hitting that spot.

"Yes. You. Did." She clung to him, her fingers digging into his arms as her body tightened around his.

"I...love...you." He emphasized each word with a hard thrust before fucking her faster.

"Yes." She wrapped her arms around his neck, clinging to him with every fiber of her being—her body, her heart, and her soul as her world exploded.

"Annie," he groaned as he buried himself deep inside of her again and again before his body shook with his release.

CHAPTER 32: Patrick

Patrick held Annie close, feeling right for the first time in too long. He kissed the top of her head, and she snuggled closer, her fingers stroking across his chest. She'd thought he was losing interest because he'd been distant after sex. He wasn't going to ever make that mistake again. It'd almost cost him everything he'd ever wanted. "I love you."

"Hmm." It was barely a sound. She was falling asleep on him.

"Look at me." He shifted to his side so he could see her face.

Her eyes fluttered open, and she smiled.

His heart almost burst. He felt so much for her—love, lust, friendship. She was his everything. "I love you." This time the words slipped from his lips, soft and reverent.

"I love you too." She touched his face and then kissed him gently.

"Promise that this"—he waved his hand—"won't happen again."

"I can't. We are definitely having sex again." Her eyes sparkled with mischief.

"I'm serious." They'd both almost ruined everything by not talking to one another.

"I promise." The sparkle left her eyes. "I'll be honest with you, but you have to be honest with me too."

"I will." He cupped her face. "I can't lose you."

"I can't lose you either." Her brown eyes filled with tears, but there were shadows in the dark depths.

"You have to tell me what you want, no matter what." He ran his hands down her shoulders, loving how soft her skin was.

She nodded.

That wasn't good enough. "Talk to me, Annie. Please." His eyes searched hers, and she glanced away. "Damn it, tell me what's wrong."

"I-I.... Sometimes, I don't want to say anything because I know I can be bossy and pushy and—"

"You can be, but I love that about you."

"You...you do?" Her eyes met his again.

"Yes."

"Really?" There was disbelief in her tone. "Even when I look at the files that you leave lying all over the house?"

"Okay." He sighed. "I don't *love* that, but I love you." He kissed her. "And I love that I never have to wonder how you feel. I love that you care so much that you want what's best for everyone."

"Even if they don't want it? Like Vic."

"Yes." He sighed again. "I wish you could understand that he needs to get away from all of us."

"I'm sorry, but I don't agree. He needs family."

"He has family. He knows he has you and your brothers. Me and Ethan. But he needs space."

"He had plenty of space before when he left. That didn't go so well, did it?"

He had to try and make her understand. "That was different. He had things to work out, and he's done that. He's gone to therapy. He's not doing drugs."

"Now, but he might slip. Have a bad day and—"

"We all have bad days."

"Yeah, be we aren't all recovering addicts."

"You're right, but—"

"And I'm right about him needing to stay here. He needs someone when he has that bad day."

"He has his sponsor."

"He needs his family."

"He needs what he says he needs." His temper was slipping so he took a deep breath. "I know you love him. I know you're scared for him, but"—he touched her lips to shut her up—"he's a grown man. He knows what is best for him better than you do."

"I disagree." Her jaw clenched like she was trying to keep from saying more.

"If he thinks this is what he needs then we have to support him." He knew she was scared, but he just didn't understand how she could be so thickheaded.

"I can't." Her jaw jutted out. "I won't. I'll love him no matter what, and I'll be there if he needs me, but I cannot support this."

"I wish I knew what to say to make you understand." He closed his eyes for a second, not wanting to continue, but he had to make sure she understood. "I'm sorry, but I have to support him with this decision."

"I'm done talking about this." She rolled away from him and got out of bed.

"Where are you going?" His eyes roamed over her ass as she walked across the room.

"Home." She picked up her clothes.

"Why?" He sat up.

"Because I don't want to stay here when we're fighting."

"We don't have to be fighting."

"And yet, we are." She started putting on her clothes.

"We wouldn't be if you'd...." He shut his mouth before making things worse.

"If I'd what? Agree with you?" She gave him the death glare.

"No." Yes, actually that'd be perfect.

"Then what?" Her foot tapped on the floor.

"If you'd just listen to me."

"Listen? Hmm." She touched her lip with her finger. "When should I have listened?" She kept going without giving him a chance to speak. "You can't mean tonight because I did listen. I just don't agree with you. So maybe you mean I should've listened before you gave Vic the money." Her face scrunched up.

He pulled on his pants and shirt, cringing inwardly as he waited for the blow.

"But you can't mean that because you didn't talk to me about it." She raised a brow, staring at him accusingly.

"I didn't talk to you because I knew you wouldn't agree with me, and we'd fight."

"We're fighting anyway." She put on her shoes and grabbed her purse.

"Good point." He took her arm.

She yanked away from him. "We're living together. He's my brother. You should've talked to me." She strode toward the door.

"I figured it was better to ask for forgiveness than permission—which you wouldn't have given." He followed her.

"You don't need my permission." She shot him a disgusted look. "It's your money. Do whatever you want with it. You're going to anyway."

"That's right. It is, and I will." That should've made him feel righteous in his decision, but instead it just made him feel empty.

CHAPTER 33: Patrick

Patrick stared at the ceiling of their bedroom, his arm around Annie who was snuggled against his side. She'd fallen asleep on the other side of the bed but had sought him out in her sleep. He did the same with her. No matter where he fell asleep, he always woke with some part of his body touching hers.

It was like in their subconscious they knew what was important. What really mattered. His hand glided gently up and down her back. He'd never felt like this with anyone. He'd thought he'd been in love before, but those feelings had been like the heat from a lamp compared to the sun. She was his everything, and he'd do anything for her...or almost anything.

He couldn't change his mind about giving Vic the money. His friend needed it. He hoped Annie would understand one day. If she didn't, it wouldn't be the only time that they'd disagree about major things, but they'd work it out. Tonight, had proven that as long as they talked to each other, they'd be okay. They'd fight. They'd disagree, but they'd be okay.

He should be sleeping as soundly as she was. He usually felt relaxed and right when he was holding her—like everything was how it was supposed to be—but tonight he was unsettled. He replayed the evening in his mind, deciphering their argument over and over and trying to figure out what it was that kept him awake. Then it hit him. It wasn't their disagreement over Vic that bothered him; it was her comment about the money.

It was his money, but he didn't want it to be, not like that. He wanted more. He looked around the room. They'd been living together for a while now, but the furniture was all his from before she'd moved in. She had some stuff on the dresser and her clothes, of course, but not much else in his house had changed. It was like she was a temporary roommate, and that didn't work for him, not anymore.

CHAPTER 34: Annie

Annie pulled her car into the garage next to Patrick's. That was odd. He usually worked later than she did unless she had an evening event. She got out of the car, grabbing the containers that were left over from the office party she'd catered that afternoon.

She had sandwiches and other finger foods. It wasn't a perfect dinner, but it'd have to do for tonight. Her feet hurt, and she was just tired. She'd thought things with her and Patrick had been settled that night they'd spent at the Club a few weeks ago, and they had...kind of.

She was still upset that he'd given Vic the money, and it'd been hard saying goodbye to her brother last week. It seemed like he'd just come back into her life, and now, he was gone again. Part of her understood that he needed this and more importantly, Patrick had needed to help Vic. What bothered her was the way Patrick had been looking at her lately. She couldn't explain it, but there was an uneasiness about him that put her instincts on alert.

Sex was great, as always, and he was definitely not distant anymore. Some nights they'd snuggle on the couch or in bed and talk for hours. At those moments everything seemed perfect, but later she'd catch him watching her with a question in his eyes.

She opened the door to the house, smiling at Sophie and Boomer's barks of joy. "Something smells good." She patted the dogs as she followed the scent of homemade bread into the kitchen. She stopped, taking in the scene.

Patrick cooked occasionally but never like tonight. He wore black slacks that hugged his ass and a dark green shirt that matched his eyes. Suddenly, she was hungry for more than food. She wanted to jump this man.

"Hey." Patrick smiled at her as he closed the oven door and straightened.

"Hi." Her heart melted at the happiness in his gaze. No one could look at another person like that and be unhappy with their relationship. All her doubts had to be in her mind. "What are you making? It smells wonderful."

"My mom's stew and homemade bread." He walked across the kitchen, taking the containers of leftovers from her. "Let me put these away."

"I love that stew." It was amazing—rich, flavorful, and rustic. "One day, I'm going to convince you to give me that recipe."

"Hmm." He put the food in the refrigerator and closed the door. "We should talk about that."

"About the recipe? Are you going to give it to me?" She almost jumped with joy. She was such a nerd when it came to food. "My clients will love this, especially on those cold and rainy fall and winter days."

"I might give it to you." He gave her that odd look again but then it quickly disappeared. "Why don't you go and change. I'll finish up in here and meet you in the living room."

"You *might* give it to me?" She was going to ignore that look. It was probably because his mother didn't want the recipe to leave the family. She'd take his mind off that little detail. She strolled over to him, unbuttoning her blouse. "What do I need to do to convince you to hand over the goods? And think before you answer because I will do"—she licked her lips and let her gaze drop to the front of his pants—"anything."

CHAPTER 35: Patrick

Patrick wanted to pull his hair out. Actually, he wanted to launch himself across the room, rip Annie's clothes off, and fuck her on the kitchen table, but that was not the plan. He wanted tonight to be perfect. "Stop." He took a step back, away from temptation.

"Stop?" Her brow wrinkled in confusion as her fingers stilled, her blouse halfway undone.

"Ah...yeah." He couldn't pull his eyes away from where she'd exposed more of her cleavage. Her breasts were large, and he knew they'd be so soft and smooth. His dick stiffened. They'd smell of perfume, warmed by her skin. Fuck him. He wanted her, but he backed away. "Go." He flipped his hand. "I'll put on some music, pour you a glass of wine, and meet you in the living room."

"Okay. Couch it is"—she smiled slightly as her eyes raked over his body, sending all the blood rushing to his cock—"but I think right here would be fun." She turned, running her fingernail across the top of the table.

He shivered as memories of those fingers scraping gently across his body threatened to make him forget that he had a mission tonight, a very important mission.

"But you're the boss." She grinned wickedly at him. "For now." She walked toward the door, letting her blouse slide down her body and then stopping for a moment to remove her skirt. She glanced at him. "I'll be on the couch. Don't keep me waiting."

"Fuck." He groaned and took several deep breaths, trying to get his dick under control. It was easier to focus now that she wasn't in eyesight, but as soon as he walked into the living room, his cock would lead the way. Then his plans would be tossed aside for a romp on the sofa. "Annie," he called out.

"Yes, dear." There was a teasing tone to her voice.

"Put some clothes on."

"What?" The teasing tone was gone.

"Please."

"You want me to get dressed?"

He didn't want to hurt her feelings. He peeked his head out of the kitchen so he could see her. "Just for a minute...."

She sat on the couch, her lush body completely bare.

His mouth went dry, and he cleared his throat. "Maybe not even a minute." He'd wanted his proposal to be romantic. Something she'd remember with a smile on her face for the rest of her life, but fast could be romantic, right?

"Is everything okay?" She pulled a pillow from the sofa and put it in front of her.

"Yes. It's perfect. I just want to talk to you."

"Talk? You want to talk. Now?" Her beautiful brown eyes filled with worry.

"About the recipe. It'll only take a minute." His eyes raked over her as his fingers dug into the wall by the door, stopping himself from rushing into the living room and launching himself on top of her.

"Okay. Fine." She stood, her eyes still full of worry.

"Seriously, as soon as I tell you...uhm, about the recipe, I am jumping you. So be prepared."

"Promise?" She smiled at him, the worry slipping away with her grin.

"You'd better believe it," he almost growled.

"I do want the recipe, but I'd be okay with waiting." She let the pillow drop to the floor.

"No." His jaw clenched. "Recipe first." The timer dinged. "I'll get the bread out of the oven and meet you in the living room."

CHAPTER 36: Annie

Okay, Annie wasn't crazy; Patrick was. She pulled on a pair of shorts. She had no idea what was going on with him. Getting his mom's stew recipe wasn't that important. It'd be nice to have it, but she'd wanted it since the first time she'd tasted it months ago. She put on a bra and T-shirt. This couldn't be just about the food. Something else was going on, but she had no idea what. Patrick had never turned down sex...until now. Usually, that'd be a huge sign that something was wrong, except the way he'd looked at her had been hot enough to almost make her melt into a puddle of mush.

She was done being the only one confused. She dug in her drawer for her little "fuck-me" shorts. The ones that had driven him nuts when they'd first met, and he'd been trying to stay away from her because of her brother. She tossed the other shorts aside and pulled these on before yanking off her shirt and bra. She grabbed a tank top that was a little too big and fell off her shoulders. With the right tip of her body, he'd get an eyeful of boob.

She brushed her teeth, washed off her makeup, added some suck-my-dick red lipstick and grinned as she pulled her hair up in a ponytail. She was ready for round two.

CHAPTER 37: Patrick

Patrick turned off the oven and pulled out the bread, sitting it on the stove. He put the lid on the stew to keep it warm. His plans had been to greet Annie with wine and romance, ask her to marry him, eat dinner, and then make love, but by the look in her eyes when she'd greeted him in the kitchen, making love was going to jump in front of dinner which was more than fine with him.

He headed into the living room. He turned on some slow and sexy music and then dimmed the lights. The ambiance was perfect. He walked to the bar and poured her a glass of her favorite wine.

"I'm ready for the recipe." Annie strolled from their bedroom.

Patrick almost dropped the glass as all the blood rushed to his cock. She wore those fuck-me shorts that he loved and with that lipstick all he could see was her on her knees, swallowing his dick.

"Are you ready to *give it* to me?" She walked up to him, letting her fingers skim across his hand as she took the glass.

"Uh...." He didn't have enough blood in his brain to form a sentence.

She took a sip of her drink, her eyes locking with his, just like she did when she sucked his dick. She licked her lips and then put the glass aside. "You're all dressed up." She ran her fingernail down his chest. "I'd say...overdressed."

"Annie...." It was a guttural groan as that damn hand of hers skimmed across his erection.

"Patrick." Her fingers slipped into his pants as she started to undo his button.

"No." He grabbed her wrist, but the softness of her skin made him even harder. He dropped her hand and stumbled backward. Damn it. He was going to get his ring on her finger before he fucked her. He didn't want his proposal to be after sex. He needed her to know that him wanting her for his wife wasn't some satiated blunder of words. "Sit. Go to the couch and sit." He moved behind a chair.

"What is wrong with you?" Her eyes flashed with anger, but there was a hint of hurt and confusion in their dark depths.

"Nothing. I'm sorry." He ran his hand through his hair. "It's just.... Please, just sit. I need to talk to you."

CHAPTER 38: Annie

"I think this is a good time for you to tell me what's going on." Annie turned and strode to the couch, refusing to freak out about Patrick's *I need to talk to you comment.* There was no way he was dumping her. They'd worked out their main issue a few weeks ago which meant it was something else. She sat. "Are you sure you're okay?"

"I'm fine." He walked over to her and handed her the glass of wine. "At least, I think I am." He smiled a little sheepishly. "You're going to make that decision."

"I'm not in the mood for riddles. Are you sick?"

"Huh?" He gave her an odd look.

"If you're sick, just tell me. We'll figure it out." Panic began to claw at her insides.

"No. I'm not sick."

"Thank God." The tension fled her body, but her relief was quickly replaced by annoyance. "Then what's going on?" She took a gulp of her wine.

"Sorry. I'm messing this up." He ran his hand through his hair again. He only did that when he was stressed or exasperated with her.

"Messing up what? Sex? Yeah, you are. I mean, you did."

"No. Not sex." He sat by her and took her hand. "I want to talk to you about my mom's recipe."

"The recipe? Seriously?" She wanted to strangle him. They could be having sex now, but instead he wanted to discuss stew. It was good but not that good.

"Yeah." His finger stroked across the skin of her hand. "It's been in my family for centuries. My great, great, great grandmother brought it over when she left Ireland for the United States."

"That's lovely." She wanted to be supportive, but this story would've been better after sex.

"No one outside of my family has it." He grinned a little. "Before we're taught how to make the stew, we have to swear that we won't give the recipe to anyone who isn't family. My mother takes this very seriously."

"Oh. I understand." Great, now she was disappointed about not jumping him, and a little sad about not getting the recipe.

"I don't think you do." He stared at her like he expected her to say something.

"No. I do. It's fine. Your mom told me that it was a family recipe when I asked her for it. I get it. If I'd known you were so serious about keeping it in the family, I wouldn't have asked you for it again. My customers would love it, but my business will survive without it." She smiled at him.

"That's what you're not getting. I'm going to give you the recipe on one condition." He kissed her hand.

"One condition? What are you...?" All the words fled as he got off the couch and onto one knee. *OMG. OMG. OMG.* Her brain screamed and jumped for joy, but she sat as still as a statue—frozen with hope.

"Annie Argotos." He pulled a ring box from his pocket and opened it. "Will you do me the honor, the privilege, the...." His face scrunched up. "Damn it, I forgot what comes next." He reached into his other pocket and pulled out a piece of paper.

"Patrick. Please, just ask me." Her words were so soft she wasn't sure if he heard her until he looked at her, his eyes overflowing with love.

"Will you marry me?"

CHAPTER 39: Patrick

Patrick was pretty sure every cell in his body stopped working as he waited for Annie's answer. It was probably only a few seconds, but to him it felt like hours. She was so still. Annie was never still. Fuck. Had he asked too soon? What if she wasn't ready to marry him or never wanted to marry him? Panic twisted in his gut. He didn't think he could come back from this. If she didn't say yes, he wasn't sure he could keep living with her.

"Yes. Yes. Yes." Her eyes filled with tears.

That was the most beautiful word he'd ever heard. It made his world right and…. "Oomph," he grunted as she launched herself off the couch and into his arms. "Annie."

He tried to keep his balance, but then the dogs joined in, licking, and jumping on both of them. He wrapped his arms around her, protecting her as they fell backward.

"Yes." She kissed him, leaning up on his chest. "Yes. I will marry you." She kissed him again. "I love you."

He grabbed her face. "I love you too." He kissed her softly, showing her everything he felt, but there was too much love to be contained in something so sweet. He deepened the kiss as he rolled over, positioning her beneath him.

Her tongue met his as she moaned against his lips, her hands tearing at his clothes.

He didn't have time for finesse. He undid his pants, his fingers pushing her little shorts aside and stroking across her pussy. "You're so wet." And ready. That was the best part because he didn't have the patience to wait to claim her. She was his. Really his. Technically, she wasn't yet, but she'd agreed, and he'd hold her to that verbal contract.

"Please." She grabbed his dick, running her hand up and down his length.

"Fuck." He pushed her hands aside and positioned himself at her entrance. He shoved inside of her in one hard thrust. She gasped, her body clamping around his cock like she'd been made just for him. "God, you feel so good."

"I love you." She whispered, her brown eyes glassy with passion.

"Say it again." He rocked into her.

"I love you." Her fingers dug into his arms.

"No, say you'll marry me. That you'll be my wife." He needed to hear it again, to know that soon a fight wouldn't be enough for her to leave him, at least not for good. They'd have to go to court for that.

She touched his cheeks, her fingers drifting to his lips. "Yes, I'll marry you, Patrick Westman."

"You're mine, Annie. Forever."

"And you're mine." She rocked against him as he pumped into her again and again, clinging to him as he claimed her as his in the most natural way there was.

CHAPTER 40: Annie

Annie lay in Patrick's arms, more content and happier than she could remember ever being. She could stay like this forever. In his arms was where she wanted to be, where she belonged.

He captured her hand and kissed it, his brow furrowing. "You're missing something."

"What?" She wasn't missing anything. Everything was perfect. He was going to be her husband.

"This is not going to work for me." He kissed her ring finger. "I want the world to know that you're mine."

"What?" she repeated. Her brain was mush from all the excitement and her orgasm, but then it hit her. "My ring." She yanked her hand from his and sat up. "Where's my ring?" She started patting his pants pockets because neither of them had bothered to remove their clothes.

"I don't know." He sat up, laughing at her. "I lost track of everything when you ambushed me."

"Ambushed?" She shot him a playful glare. "I didn't hear you complaining at the time." She shoved his shoulder. "Help me find my ring."

"Whatever you want, soon-to-be Mrs. Westman." He kissed her.

"Annie Westman. I like the sound of that," she whispered against his lips but then pulled away. "But I want to see the ring."

"Here it is." He picked it up from the floor and pulled it from the box.

She held out her hand and he slid it onto her finger. "It's beautiful." It was a pear-shaped diamond with smaller diamonds around it.

"Do you really like it? If you don't, we can—"

She touched his lips, stopping his words. "I love it. It's perfect." She kissed him again.

"I'm glad." He stuffed his dick back in his pants and zipped up before wrapping his arms around her and taking them both to the couch. "Nick and I spent forever finding the right one. He thought you might want to pick it out yourself." He hesitated. "Would you rather do that?"

"No." She curled against his side. "I'm glad you picked it out for me."

"Really?" He studied her face.

"Yes." She held out her hand, staring at the ring. "Every time I look at it, I'll think of you and how you thought of me while you picked it out."

"I wanted this proposal to be perfect." He frowned. "I had it all planned. I knew I should've taken you out to dinner, but then I thought of the recipe and—"

"It was perfect." She leaned up and kissed him. "Everything was perfect."

"Thanks, but the quick bang on the floor isn't the romantic gesture I was going for."

"Romance is overrated sometimes, and the rest was romantic."

"I wanted this to be a story you could share with our kids and grandkids."

"It is." She'd be telling this story to everyone, but she may leave out some parts.

"Not all of it."

"Sure, I will...eventually. When they're young, I'll tell them the romantic stuff and smile as I remember the hot, rough, fuck on the floor. When they're older I'll gross them out by telling them that part, without the details of course."

"Make sure you tell them that you jumped me." He laughed.

"Oh, definitely. I want our daughters to understand that letting a man know exactly what you want is perfectly fine."

"Our daughters are not going to have sex, ever."

She snorted. "They will, but we'll all love you enough to let you pretend that they don't."

"Good." He pulled her closer.

"What about when they have our grandkids?"

"Immaculate conception." He smiled against the top of her head.

"And the boys?" She looked up at him.

"I'll get them a membership to the Club." His eyes sparkled with challenge.

"Then the girls will get a membership too." She sat up. "There will not be any double standards about sex with our kids."

"Babe, we can argue about the sex lives of our unconceived children later." He grabbed her ponytail. "Right now, I think I have a fiancé to fuck."

"You just fucked her." She undid his pants, more than ready for round two.

"That didn't count. You weren't wearing my ring." He shoved her shirt up and over her head.

"But I'd agreed to marry you, so it does count."

"I disagree." He bent, pulling one of her nipples into his mouth and sucking.

Her body throbbed with need, and she clutched his head, keeping him in place. "Disagree if you want, but I know you haven't gotten a blow job from your fiancé yet."

"And I haven't gotten to taste her pussy." He shoved her down on the couch and yanked off her shorts. "I bet my fiancé's pussy tastes even better than my girlfriend's."

"You'll have to let me know." She opened her legs, putting one on his shoulder, waiting for the beginning of her lifetime of pleasure with the love of her life.

****

Thanks for reading **More Than a Voyeur**. I hope you enjoyed this part of Patrick and Annie's story. If you did, please take a moment to leave a review.

If you haven't read how Patrick and Annie meet, you can get the first book in that series for free. https://books2read.com/u/bxqBMk

If you have read The Voyeur series, you can get to know the other men and women of La Petite Mort Club. I have several first in series free. You can find them on my website at: https://ellisoday.com/series/free-books/

Plus, if you sign up for my newsletter, you can get the entire Six Nights of Sin series for free (all six nights of Nick and Sarah's contract—every delicious fantasy) as a thank you gift.

Go to my website or email me for details:
https://www.ellisoday.com/
authorEllisOday@gmail.com
Six Nights of Sin is also available for free in audiobook when you join my
newsletter.
https://dl.bookfunnel.com/vi2abq0qo3
If you want to read the stories before they are published, follow me on Ream.
You'll get access to my work(s) in progress as I write them.
http://www.reamstories.com/EllisODay

Free - His Sub

Terry wandered through the crowd of well-dressed women and men at La Petite Mort Club. It was the same scene every time Ethan, his friend and owner of the Club, threw one of these events. The members mingled with the newbies, hoping to snag something different or someone interesting.

Ethan strolled casually toward him, a ready smile on his face as he greeted his guests. "Terry, about time you made it down here."

"Like you can talk." His friend spent most of his time in the back office, watching the Club on monitors.

"I've been mingling for over an hour."

"It's your business not mine." He leaned against the balustrade, peering down on the crowd.

"True, but you could sell your practice and buy me out."

"And run this place?" He laughed. "No thank you." He tossed back his scotch. "I spend enough time here as it is." He used to practically live here except when he was at the office or in court, but lately he'd been staying home more.

"Good turn out tonight." Ethan waved at a waitress and a moment later they each had another drink.

"Yeah, but I don't see one interesting person in this crop of wannabe members."

"And you can tell if someone is interesting just by looking at them?"

"I can tell not one of them has an original thought. Look at them. They're all in red." The Club was awash in a sea of red dresses—short, long, dark, light but always red.

"It is a Valentine's Day party."

"I know but you'd think one woman"—he held up his finger—"one would consider that everyone else would be in red and wear a different color."

"There are some pinks out there."

"Same thing, just lighter."

Ethan grabbed his phone from his pocket and looked at the text, frowning.

"Problem?" The Club was usually a safe place but on open night events, when Ethan allowed non-members access in order to recruit new members, the place could get dangerous.

"A little skirmish over a woman." Ethan grinned, his blue eyes sparkling as a couple of young guys hurried past them, almost tripping in their haste to stay close to a group of very attractive women. "These youngsters haven't learned that sharing is more fun."

He ignored Ethan's teasing. He'd taken a lot of shit from Ethan, Nick and even Patrick because he wasn't into the sharing thing. He preferred it to be him and one woman, one sweet, little sub. Since he was in no mood to listen to any more crap, he'd change the subject. "Those kids barely look old enough to drink."

"You're showing your age." Ethan patted his shoulder. "You should find some nice, young thing and teach her how to please her master."

"Maybe I will, if any of them show enough originality to dress in something other than red."

"I've got to go and sort out this problem." Ethan slid his phone into his pocket. "I'll find you later. If you find that elusive non-red dress, I'd suggest we share but...." He chuckled as he headed down the stairs, maneuvering through the crowd like he had nowhere to go, when in reality he was heading for the back—the playrooms.

Terry's eyes stopped and lingered on the new hire, Desiree, who was moving around the room, talking and flirting with all the men and some women. She was interesting—exotic and smart—but there was a shrewdness behind her eyes that he'd learned a long time ago to avoid. A woman like her had an agenda and she stuck with it, no matter what.

Someone slammed into his back, causing his drink to spill down his front, staining his shirt and suit.

"Oh…oh, I'm so sorry."

He spun around and encountered a red dress and breasts—milky white and lush. The skin would be fragrant and softer than rose petals.

"Oh. Your shirt. Let me get something to wipe that up."

He forced his eyes away from those lovely breasts. Her hair was a rich mahogany. It'd probably hang past her shoulders in waves of curly silk but right now it was piled haphazardly on her head in what had been some kind of elegant style before disobedient strands had escaped their restraint. She looked mussed and damnit, he wanted to be the one to muss her.

"Paper towels? Napkins?" She glanced around and then hurried over to the bar.

She was short and curvy—her body succulent, ripe and he'd bet juicy. She grabbed a stack of napkins and headed for him. Her dress was too tight, like she'd recently gained some weight. He usually went for the tall, athletic types but for some reason his dick had picked this woman.

She returned to his side and dabbed at the wetness on his shirt and jacket as if she actually gave a shit about his clothes. This was no subtle caress, no flirtation—just indifferent efficiency.

"I'm so sorry." She wadded the napkins in her hand, still patting at his clothes.

"You said that already." His words came out gruffer than he'd meant. No one treated him with disinterest. He was a rich, successful, attractive man and she was treating him like a child. He wanted to pull up her—unfortunately, red—dress and fuck her right here. They were at the Club. It wasn't out of the question.

Her hand froze. "Oh." Her large hazel eyes looked startled and then hurt. "Sorry. Ah, excuse me." She headed toward the stairs, dropping the wet napkins in the trash before disappearing in the crowd.

He turned around, so he could see the first floor and waited for her to appear. She hurried across the downstairs room, bumping and stumbling through the crowd. A lone, scared, little rabbit in a room full of predators. She stopped for a moment, scanning the crowd as if searching for someone.

"Who are you looking for, little rabbit?" he mumbled to himself. "A husband? Boyfriend?" He grinned as he lifted his scotch to his lips. "Girlfriend?" He frowned at the empty glass. "You spilled my drink. I'll forgive you, but it's going to cost you." He waved at one of the waitresses. "Everything has a price, little rabbit." As one of the best divorce lawyers in town, he knew that better than anyone.

The waitress brought him another drink. He paid, giving her a large tip before turning to find his little rabbit. He took a sip of the scotch, enjoying the smooth burn and his lush little bunny's journey through La Petite Mort Club. She froze in her tracks, her jaw dropping open as she gazed at a threesome on one of the couches.

The woman was sandwiched between two men, stroking one's cock as the other man fondled her beneath her red dress. The man behind her looked up and said something to the little rabbit. Her face heated and Terry's eyes dropped to her chest. Yep, they were a pretty shade of pink but what he really wanted to know was if the color matched her pussy.

She stumbled away from the threesome, bumping into another man. It was Richard, who stopped her from falling and then immediately let her go, stepping away. She was safe with Richard. As a member of the Club and a gentleman, he knew that safewords were law and consent was absolutely necessary. She said something to Richard and continued through the Club, disappearing in the crowd.

"You're not getting away that easily." He followed along on the upper floor, keeping her in sight. He had no idea why but he wanted her. Maybe it was simply because she was different than everyone else here.

He took another sip of his drink. It was obviously the little rabbit's first time at a place like this but she didn't seem eager to participate or interested in watching. She truly seemed to be looking for someone specific—not just someone to fuck. Well, she'd found the latter because he was going to fuck her. In the office he followed his head but at La Petite Mort Club his cock was king.

She headed toward the playrooms. There was no way he was going to miss this. He sauntered down the stairs, grabbing another drink on the way. She wasn't hard to follow. She left a path of irritated people in her wake as she bumped into them and apologized profusely before hurrying forward. Her full, round hips swayed under her tight, red dress that'd seen better days—hem frayed and at least five years out of style. Not that he minded, especially the snug fit of the cloth, but his women were usually much more put together.

They were the CEO types—women who thrived on being in charge. He enjoyed teaching them how much fun turning over control could be. When they were with him, he was their dom, their master and he made sure they loved every second. He told them when to kneel, when to suck, when to spread their legs or ass and when to come. The more power they had in their everyday life the more they craved bowing to his wishes. His little rabbit wouldn't know what power was. She was a hot mess of a woman. Still, his dick wanted her, so his dick would have her.

She was hurrying out of the first playroom when he entered the hallway. Her eyes were huge and her cheeks were on fire. She ducked into the next room and quickly came out—even redder than before.

"Excuse me." He'd offer his assistance in her search. She'd be grateful. He could capitalize on that unless she was looking for her husband or boyfriend. He wasn't in the mood to share. He would, however, allow the other man to watch. He could give the guy some pointers on how to take care of his wife because this woman obviously needed guidance.

"You?" Her eyes narrowed.

That wasn't the reaction he was used to. Women usually purred for him.

"Are you following me?"

"What would you do if I said I was?" He took a step toward her.

"I'd scream. There are bouncers here. I saw them."

Lord, she was cute. "Yes, but if they came running at every little scream they'd die of exhaustion."

As if to emphasis his point a woman screamed in ecstasy. His little rabbit's face heated and she averted her gaze.

"Who are you looking for?" He ran his finger lightly down her cheek. Her skin was as smooth as porcelain but much warmer and softer.

"Ah..." Her breath hitched, making her breasts swell dangerously above her gown.

He could have her out of it in a minute. The skin would be even softer than that on her face. "Did you lose your husband?"

"No." She licked her lips.

There was no way he could let that offer pass. He slowly bent, giving her time to refuse him. He may command his women but he made sure they always wanted it first. Her eyes dropped to his mouth and he couldn't help a slight smirk. She wanted this as much as he did. He moved closer and let his lips rest gently on hers. He'd take it slow, make her yearn for him and then he'd make her obey.

"What are you doing?" She turned her head.

"Kissing you." His lips brushed against her cheek. He wasn't about to lose ground.

"Why?" She turned again, her eyes meeting his.

The confusion in her hazel gaze was as obvious as the hideous dress on her gorgeous body. She may remind him of a rabbit but she couldn't be that naive. She had to be in her mid to late thirties.

He should use flowery words—tell her she was beautiful, desirable—but that wasn't him. Blunt was the kindest word to describe him. "Because, I want to."

"You don't even know me."

He was losing ground. The interest in her face was being replaced with disgust. "No, but I know I want you." Damn, he shouldn't have said that.

"Well, too bad." She pushed on his chest and he stepped back, letting her pass.

"This is a sex club, you know." He followed. "If you aren't here for sex, why are you here?"

She spun around. "I'm quite aware of what this place is and just because I don't want you, a stranger to...to"—she waved her hand about—"in the hallway."

He laughed. "We wouldn't be the first. There are people fucking in the main room."

"I know. I saw." Her cheeks heated.

He stepped closer. "You are adorable." He touched a strand of hair that was resting on her shoulder. It was like satin.

"I'm a mess." She pulled her hair free from his fingers.

"A hot mess. A fiery, hot, sexy mess." He moved closer with every other word. "One I want to fuck, right now."

Her eyes hardened. "Too bad because I don't"—again she waved her hand about—"you know, with strangers in the hallway." She shoved his chest again.

He took a small step back but he wasn't giving up yet. "We can go to a private room."

"No."

Shit. By the look on her face, he'd just made a bigger blunder.

"Let me go." She pushed him again.

Damn. She'd said the worst three words in the English language besides I love you. He moved away, releasing her for the moment. "Sorry."

She harrumphed.

"I made a mistake."

"Yes, you did." She hurried down the hallway but not before he'd seen the look of hurt in her large eyes.

"What the fuck do you want from me? I made a mistake and apologized." He trailed after her.

"I want you to leave me alone. Please. Go away."

He stopped. His little rabbit was running but perhaps, he shouldn't chase. She darted down a hallway toward the hardcore BDSM rooms.

Normally, she'd be fine—embarrassed but fine. Except with all the newbies here, tonight wasn't a normal night. He hurried after her. "Hey, I don't think you want to go—"

"Leave me alone." She walked faster. "I need to find my friend and get out of here."

"Okay, but I don't—"

"Go away." She sounded both mad and as if she were going to cry.

"Suit yourself, but I warned you."

She strode into the closest room. He should leave. Let her find out that he wasn't the worst thing in a place like this, not in a long shot, but his feet followed her. She was his little rabbit. He'd found her. No one else was going to enjoy her until he'd had his taste.

"Vicky? Vicky? Are you in here?"

He stepped into the room, staying in the shadows. She was looking around in the dark for her friend. It only took a moment for one of the six guys to notice the little rabbit who'd stumbled into their den.

"Shit," he mumbled. Not one of those guys was a regular.

Grab your free copy and find out what happens next.[1]
https://books2read.com/u/3nKw7B

COMING SOON:

ETHAN'S STORY
MATTIE'S STORY
JAKE'S STORY
REBECCA AND DEREK'S STORY
VIC'S STORY
See All Of My Books On my website
https://ellisoday.com/books/
All Audiobooks
https://ellisoday.com/genre/audiobooks/

If you want to read the stories before they are published, follow me on Ream.
You'll get access to my work(s) in progress as I write them.
https://reamstories.com/ellisoday
For film and TV rights inquiries: AuthorEllisODay@EllisODay.com
Email me with questions, concerns or to let me know what you thought of the
book. I love hearing from readers.
authorEllisOday@gmail.com

https://www.EllisODay.com
Follow me
Facebook
https://www.facebook.com/EllisODayRomanceAuthor/
Closed FB Group (sneak peeks, sample chapters, and other bonuses)
https://www.facebook.com/groups/ellisodaysteamyromance/
Bookbub
https://www.bookbub.com/authors/Ellis-o-day

Instagram

https://www.instagram.com/authorEllisOday/[1]

Twitter
https://twitter.com/Ellis_o_day

Pinterest
www.pinterest.com\AuthorEllisODay[2]

---

1. https://www.instagram.com/authorellisoday/

2. http://www.pinterest.com/AuthorEllisODay

Don't miss out!

Visit the website below and you can sign up to receive emails whenever Ellis O. Day publishes a new book. There's no charge and no obligation.

https://books2read.com/r/B-A-WMME-SFFHD

BOOKS 2 READ

Connecting independent readers to independent writers.

Also by Ellis O. Day

Hot Holidays
The Mistletoe Game
A Banging New Year
Cupid's Misfire

La Petite Mort Club
Six Nights of Sin
The Voyeur Series Books 1 - 4
Six Weeks of Seduction
A Merry Masquerade For Christmas
The Dom's Submission Series (Parts 1-3)
Hot Holidays
The Billionaire's Baby

La Petite Mort Club Intimate Encounters
His Lesson
Playing House
His Love
His Imperfect Day
More Than a Voyeur

Six Nights Of Sin
Interviewing For Her Lover
Taking Control
School Fantasy
Master-Slave Fantasy
Punishment Fantasy
The Proposition

The Billionaire's Baby
The Baby Bargain
Making the Baby
The Baby Battle
Having The Baby

The Dom's Submission
His Sub
His Mission
His Submission

The Pleasure Associate
The New Hire
Becoming a Whore
Back to the Grinding

The Voyeur
The Voyeur
Watching the Voyeur

Touching the Voyeur
Loving the Voyeur

Standalone
The Dom's Birthday Weekend